INDIANS DON'T KISS

Indians Don't Kiss

a novel

Margaret Burnett

Polygon
Edinburgh

First published by
Polygon
22 George Square
Edinburgh

Copyright © Margaret Burnett 1996

Set in Galliard by Palimpsest Book Production Limited,
Polmont, Stirlingshire
Printed and bound in Great Britain by
Cromwell Press, Broughton Gifford, Melksham, Wiltshire.

A CIP record is available for this title.

ISBN 0 7486 6212 X

The Publisher acknowledges subsidy from

THE SCOTTISH ARTS COUNCIL

towards the publication of this volume.

To Anne, Janice and Sue

1

A MAN APPROACHED, carrying a tray on his head; pausing to scratch his balls, he put the tray on the ground, squatted beside it and stared up at me. Laughing excitedly, Mum kept touching me as if she couldn't believe I was with her; Dad was telling the coolie where to put the luggage in the car. A crow flapped down heavily beside the man, scattering dust.

'What does he want?' I asked, trying to appear unconcerned.

We looked at the man who looked back at us. He waved his arm over his tray.

'Sweets, Memsahib?' he asked.

'To sell you some sweets,' Dad replied in his matter-of-fact way.

On the road, I stared out of the car window looking for signs of change in the landscape. But it was exactly as I had left it eleven years ago. 'What did you expect?' Mum asked.

'I didn't expect it to be all the same,' I said. 'Have the people not changed?'

'Not really,' Mum said. 'They'll think you have, though.' She glanced at my head.

I searched through the messy streets, the run-down little shops, and the people on the road for some sign that I had been away and had now come back. As we approached Vishnapur I searched more anxiously, but even the holes in the road seemed in the same place. The driver drove with his hand on the horn as men and women, chickens and children and dogs wandered across the road. We swerved out into the narrow road to overtake lorries as others thundered towards us, horns blaring; I felt no fear, only exhilaration. We stopped at the level-crossing on the Grand Trunk Road and a young man on a bicycle held on to the roof of the car while he waited for the gates to lift. On the other side of the car a rickshaw driver wiped his face with a tattered cloth.

'How's the rickshaw man who used to take me to school?' I asked.

'Oh, he's dead now,' Mum said, bending forward to look out of the window. 'He died a long time ago.'

The woman sitting in the rickshaw raised her arm to pull the end of her sari over her head and her glass bangles jingled. I could see her feet resting on the tin-lined bottom of the rickshaw, bare, and rough and womanly.

The car drove on to the college compound and stopped outside the wooden gate. Two women watched me get out. They pulled the ends of their saris across their mouths to hide their smiles of disbelief.

'You've come back, then?' Ganga said. 'How are you?' She was the hostel cook's wife.

'Yes, I've come back. I'm fine. How are you?' My Bengali felt thick and clumsy on my tongue.

'I'm fine,' she said, still grinning. She looked as gaunt and old as ever, but she was wearing white now, like a widow. This was for her son who had drowned in the river when the ferry capsized.

'You've cut all your hair off,' Jamuna, a college sweeper, said. 'Why have you done that? You had beautiful hair. You look like a mad woman.'

'Well,' I replied, my smile stiff on my face. 'I just did.'

'I knew they'd laugh at you,' Mum said in English. 'Don't worry about it.'

'I'm not.'

'Good.' Looking behind me, her face softened. 'Here's Sheraphuli,' she said. Unfamiliar with the name, I expected a new baby. But she was pointing to a dog.

'You've got a dog?' I asked in astonishment. I was never allowed one for fear of rabies.

'No,' Dad said. 'We haven't.' He stood by the entrance to the flats, waiting.

'She's a bazaar dog I feed sometimes.' Mum gave her a long, sad look. 'She's pregnant.'

I turned away. A wet nose touched my bare leg.

Other people drifted over expectantly, but I moved towards the flats and we went upstairs.

Mum went straight into the kitchen and bustled about; I hesitated in the sitting room. The big bright flat seemed unnaturally still and smelled faintly of damp cement. Dad was standing by the dining-room table with his hands in his pockets so I went and sat down there. A bird called from outside.

'That's a bul bul! I cried.

'Yes,' Dad said, but he probably hadn't heard it.

Mum came through the kitchen doorway carrying a cup of coffee. She put the cup down on the table in front of me.

'Would you like to move into the sitting-room?' Dad asked.

'All right,' I said.

Mum picked up my coffee.

'That's OK,' I said.

'No, no,' she said. 'I'll carry it for you.'

It wasn't a huge move. The dining-room table was at one end of the large whitewashed room and the sitting-room was at the other, with a blue carpet and shabby chairs around it. Sharp white light poured in from two verandah doors and a window.

Mum walked ahead of me and waited until I had sat down and then handed me the cup, laughing a little as she did so. 'Everyone's been asking for you,' she said. 'They all want to see you. All the students too.' She squeezed my other hand.

'Yes,' I said.

She laughed again, and her face flushed slightly as she took her hand away and went to sat down. The fan was gently lifting her fair hair off her face in little gusts.

'Did we tell you that we got money to build new servants' quarters?' Dad asked.

'No,' I said politely.

'The Germans gave us a huge cheque,' he said, settling back in his chair and folding his arms. 'So we built really good quarters, with running water and toilets, oh everything.'

'On the other side of the playing fields,' Mum said. 'In that corner by the jute mill wall.'

'Anyway, when it was built and it really is marvellous, do you know what they said?'

'No, what?'

'They said it was too good for the servants and that it should be the married students' quarters instead.'

'And is that what it is?' I asked.

'Yes,' he said shortly, his eyes aglow with his story.

'He had a big row with the Principal,' Mum said quietly.

He scratched his cheek self-consciously and then let his hands rest on the arms of the chair. 'I had to give way in the end,' he said.

There was a sudden smell of the river, dirty and enfolding. And they take all this for granted, I thought as I breathed it in. It was early in the morning, just after breakfast, that soft, promising time of day. The river with its smell was as huge and brown as ever. When they cross it in the ferries, people scoop it up in their hands and drink it, imbibing its holiness and its diseases.

When I was wee a man used to come to the school gates selling ice-cream from a little box on his bicycle. Selling dysentery, Dad said. That didn't stop me. I ate it secretly, and other things too, and I didn't get ill once in eighteen years. I played with the servants' children all the time and the only occasion I had nits in my hair was when we were on leave in Scotland. Mum and Granny laughed about that as they denitted me with the special comb. Mum had had malaria four times and Dad had jaundice once; he stepped off the boat, a young and earnest missionary and the first thing he got was chronic dysentery.

4

Dad cleared his throat as a prelude to speaking. 'How long are you staying for?' he asked. 'You didn't say in your letter.'

I looked at the floor. 'I've got a three month visitor's visa, so I thought I'd stay for three months.'

'Three months?' Mum said. 'What about your job?'

This had come up sooner than I expected. 'Well, actually, I've given it up.'

'Given it up,' she cried, dismay filling her face. 'But you loved it. You said so in your letters.'

'No, I didn't say that.'

'Yes, you did. You wrote about the children and how well they were doing and how you enjoyed your classes, and the other teachers –.'

'Wait a minute, Isabel. You've handed your notice in, Hannah. Is that right?'

'That's right.'

'And what are you going to do?'

'I don't know.'

'You don't know?' Mum cried.

'No, I don't know. I'm going to think about it while I'm here.'

'But you've been teaching for so long,' Mum said. 'Why stop now?' Her blue eyes were round with pain as she looked at me.

Dad put his cup down, uncrossed his legs and leaned towards me. 'So what *are* you going to do?'

I leaned back. 'I don't know, Dad.'

'No idea at all?'

'No.' I was smiling while he looked at me sternly. 'I've got three months to think about it.'

'I see,' he said.

I had no idea what it was he saw.

'I'm sorry you're unhappy,' Mum said.

'I'm not unhappy, Mum.'

'You will tell me if you're not happy, won't you?'

'Yes, Mum.'

They exchanged glances, Mum worried, Dad cold. He picked up his cup and took a careful sip. I glanced over his shoulder at the brightness of the day. There were voices from below, people going about their work. I caught phrases here and there, familiar words and intonations that I hadn't heard for eleven years. You forget such a lot and then it all comes rushing back. I drank my coffee to hide my tears.

'Do you remember Shankar?' Mum asked brightly. 'The sweeper's boy.'

'Of course. We played together. Bheme's son.'

'He's in jail,' she said.

'Is he? Why?'

'He stole things from the place he was working.'

'Remember you used to frisk him after he'd been here to play with me?'

Dad laughed.

'I never frisked him,' Mum said, looking embarrassed. 'I had to ask him to empty his pockets though.'

'Poor Shankar,' I said.

Dad cleared his throat. 'Did Mum write to you about Khup Lalzrom?'

'Is he the clever one?'

'I'm preparing an application form for Yale for him at the moment,' he said proudly, lifting his head and looking at the wall. Mum made a little movement with her foot. He glanced at her. 'There was a spot of trouble,' he said.

'What kind of trouble?'

'Oh, he got a girl pregnant in Mizoram, but that has been dealt with.'

He laughed apologetically. I fixed my eyes on his white, clean, sandalled feet.

'They paid her money,' Mum said quietly.

There was a silence.

'I'd like to lie down now,' I said. 'I'm very tired.'

2

I SLEPT FOR A while and woke up to murmured voices on the other side of the door. Then the door opened slowly and Mum looked in.

'Are you awake?' she asked and seeing that I was she came in. She brought with her a smell of vegetable curry and Roshan cooking in the kitchen.

'Here's Shani,' she said, tears coming into her eyes in anticipation of the reunion.

Shani peeked round the door and then came in. She'd been my ayah since I was five. She looked just the same with that defiant smile on her face, guarded but welcoming too. I sat up and she sat beside me on the bed and I wondered what to do. Indians don't kiss. But what the hell, I thought. I leaned over and put my hands on her bony shoulders and kissed the hollow of her cheek. She looked surprised and then I saw that she was struggling to hold back tears. I waited to see if the tears would fall. They didn't. She reached up and put her hand on my head and looked at Mum.

'What's this?' she said as she smoothed her hand over my bent head.

'Fashion,' Mum said quickly. 'That's the fashion now.'

'Like a widow,' Shani said. 'Why do you want to go around looking like a widow? But it's good that you're back. Your Mummy's been missing you so much.'

I looked at Mum and she laughed in an apologetic kind of way.

'How long have I been asleep?'

'About an hour.'

'Anjali's waiting for you,' Shani said.

'She didn't come with you?'

'No, she's waiting for you at the house.'

'Have I got time to go and see her before lunch?'

'Plenty of time,' Mum said.

'You'll have a lot to say,' Shani said, standing up, and the two of them stood there and looked at me.

'She's expecting me?' I said, lightly. It had been a long time. No need to rush.

'I think so,' Mum said.

'She's bought a new dress for Lucky,' Shani said as she picked up her floor brush. 'On you go now. I'll see you later, eh?' She went out of the room but Mum stayed where she was.

'I'd better go then,' I said.

'There's just one thing,' Mum said.

'What?'

'Don't talk to her about her marriage.'

'I'll see if she brings it up herself. She may want to talk about it.'

'I don't think so. Not from what Shani has been saying. And another thing.'

'Yes?'

She made me wait for a moment. Then, with an unhappy look on her face, she said, 'Don't tell her you've given up teaching.'

'Why not?'

She made me wait again, staring out of the window. 'You've had so much,' she said finally. 'And she's had nothing. You've thrown it all away and I don't think she would understand that. In fact, I know she wouldn't.'

I'd forgotten Mum's skill at delivering left hooks.

'I'll see how it goes. It'll be nice to see her again,' I said, pretending to have ducked the blow.

8

I walked towards our compound gate and Ganga asked, smiling, 'Where are you going?'

'To see Anjali,' I said, feeling shy and not stopping.

'She's going to see Anjali,' Ganga called to someone as I closed the wooden gate behind me.

I walked the hundred yards along the river to the main compound. A rickshaw bell rang behind me and I stepped out of the way. People were going home from bathing and praying; a woman in a wet sari passed me, carrying a brass gourd of holy river water. Earlier, fishermen's boats had drifted in and out of a light mist, but it had been dried by the sun. A man selling chunna choor set his tray up on a stand by the main gate. 'Chunna choor, Memsahib?' he asked hopefully. Students milled around him.

The Library, grand with doric columns and a deep portico, stood at the end of the tree-lined drive, serenely contemplating the brown river and the thick low line of green spiky palms on the other side. The main compound had been laid out by the first Baptist missionaries who came to India in the early nineteenth century; our compound was cement box mid-twentieth. Both swarmed with students, lecturers, birds, stray dogs and cows; pushed away to the edges were the servants' quarters. The College was a green oasis in this over-crowded industrial town that spewed its waste into the river, chemicals, shit, dead cows and all.

Roshan and Shani's and Anjali's house was tucked behind the massive, ornate iron gate. It looked even tinier than I remembered as I stood outside the little netted verandah. The door was open.

'Hello,' I called in English, sounding foolish and timid.

There was no reply.

'Anybody there?' I said, this time in Bengali.

Beyond the verandah was a room, and off it, a kitchen. Shani had raised five children here. The rope-strung bed was in the same place in the corner and under it, the black trunk where they kept the bedding. Another trunk stood in the opposite corner and above it were the rough wooden shelves that Shani and Anjali reached by climbing onto the trunk, pulling down battered tins they stored things in. Light streamed in from the small barred window but even so, it was a dark little room, a dense, crowded room, smelling of spices and coconut hair-oil. Sometimes, in Scotland, I'd get a whiff of masala, ghostlike, and my heart would tighten with longing for this house.

There was a movement from the side of the house and Anjali came round the corner carrying a red plastic bucket of water. A wee girl in a yellow dress followed her.

'It used to be tin,' I said to her. 'You're getting very modern. I like the red.' Calm down woman, you're havering.

'There you are,' she said. 'Come inside. Come, come.'

She went into the dark little kitchen and put the bucket in a corner and then came back into the main room. She looked older, and thinner too, but she seemed more composed than she used to be. She looked gladly up at me and wiped tears away with the end of her sari. Then she picked up the little girl. Lucky was three now and she didn't look anything like the photos that I had studied intently. She was thin and very dark, with Anjali's long, narrow face. Her eyes were suspicious and searching as she stared at me. There was no prettiness to her, no childish appeal; she was like a woman in miniature. I smiled and she hid her face in her mother's shoulder.

'Here's Auntie Hannah,' Anjali said. 'Look, here she is. Come on now, don't hide your face like that. Auntie wants to see you. Do you want to hold her? Come on, you hold her.'

I rested her angular little body on my hip.

'She's pretty,' I said. 'She looks clever too.'

'She's too thin,' Anjali said, giving the girl's leg a pinch. 'And so dark. She won't get any fairer but with luck she'll get plumper. Put her down now. You see what happens if you don't smile? Auntie will get cross.'

'No, I won't, I won't.' But I put her down and she rushed to her mother.

We sat down on the rope-strung bed and Lucky tried to climb on her mother's knee but she pushed her away.

'Why did you cut your hair?' Anjali asked. 'Have you had it like that for long? You look like a widow.'

'Not long, no. I cut it just before I came. It's the fashion. I like having no hair. I know it doesn't suit me but I thought I'd try it. It makes my face look really big, doesn't it? I think I've got past caring how I look.' She was looking at me, wondering about me; I wondered about myself too, a lot of the time.

'You look so young,' Anjali said.

'Do I?'

'Yes. How do I look?'

'Just the same.'

'I don't think so.' She stood up. 'I've got to start preparing the meal.'

I followed her into the sooty little kitchen and squatted down on the floor and Lucky squatted beside me. We watched as Anjali crumpled up paper, put twigs on top and then heavier bits of wood, and lit a match. Of course, it lit the first time. I used to try that and they'd sit beside me solemnly, Shani and Anjali, watching as I went through half a box of matches trying to get the damn thing to stay alight.

My legs quickly got stiff and I stood up and leaned against the wall. Lucky stood up too.

'Do you remember when I first came here?' I asked.

Anjali was bent low on the floor, blowing on the fire, her lips making a perfect funnel. When I tried that, all I got was smoke in my face.

'Of course,' she said, between blows.

'So do I.'

'What do you remember? '

'I remember this room. There seemed to be nothing but faces in it, all laughing at me,' I said.

'We weren't laughing at you. You just seemed strange.'

'How was I strange?'

'You were fat and wore shorts and had short yellow hair. I thought you were a boy. But it wasn't as short as it is now,' she added with a smile to the fire.

'I didn't know that. You never told me.'

11

She measured out two cups of rice and poured it on to a round brass tray. She handed the tray to me and I carried it back into the main room and sat down on the bed and began to sift through it, cleaning it of stones. Lucky followed me and stood by my knee. She grew bolder and her little hand crept towards the rice and she began to clean it too, picking daintily at the black stones.

'Do you clean rice in Scotland?' Anjali asked from the kitchen.

'No, it comes already cleaned in plastic bags.'

'That's nice.'

'Roshan brought me over, I remember, and he picked me up and sat me on the bed. Someone gave me a biscuit.'

'That was me.'

I sifted away, not paying much attention to the rice. Lucky picked out a stone I had missed. 'Do you remember that I took my shoes off?'

'You always took them off.'

'But that first day.'

'I don't remember that,' she said.

'I did it to copy you. You seemed so old and grown up and I wanted to do everything that you did. But your mother told my mother who told my father.'

I took the rice into the kitchen and put it on the floor beside the fire and then stood in the doorway with my little shadow beside me. Anjali was squatting on the floor, grinding masala between two stones, rhythmically moving her body backward and forward with the sound of stone on stone, breaking the rhythm occasionally to splash water on the mixture, until the seeds were a wet pulp. The kitchen was filled with the familiar pungent smell. She wiped the sweat off her face with the end of her sari and said,

'Was he angry?'

'It was the first time I remember him being so angry with me. He leaned right over to me that lunchtime and said that if he heard that I had taken them off again he wouldn't let me play with you. I couldn't understand why he was so angry.'

'Why was he?' She paused to look at me.

'Oh, you know – snakes, scorpions, hookworm.'

'I've had hookworm,' she said quietly. She looked at her daughter who stood beside me, shoeless. There was a silence.

'Scotland has changed you,' she said as she measured out two cups of dal onto the brass tray.

'Marriage has changed you.'

'So I am different?' She stood up with the dal and we returned to the main room. She sat on the floor with the dal and began to clean it with tremendous efficiency, flicking out little stones and pieces of wood. I sat on the bed again.

'I suppose you must be,' I said.

'It's not marriage that has changed me, it's being a mother. You should get married and have children.'

'Is marriage such a good thing?' This came out before I could stop it. All I knew about Anjali's marriage was that her husband was in the south of India. She came home to give birth to Lucky, went back to him, and then, after a short while, returned here.

'Get married and we can talk about it,' she said, concentrating on the dal.

Lucky's dusty, narrow little feet stood close to mine. 'That's not so easy,' I said.

'Do you have a boyfriend?' Anjali asked. Unlike all the other Indians I knew, Anjali didn't giggle whenever the word boyfriend was mentioned. But there was a coyness in her tone and she gave me a sly look.

'I've had boyfriends, but nobody at the moment.'

'Boyfriends, eh? All these men and no one to marry.'

'No, no one to marry.'

'Still, you're a teacher and that's a good thing. That's what I want Lucky to be. I'm going to get her educated, get her to learn everything and to go to school and college and become a teacher. She's started with a tutor and she knows her alphabet already.'

'So soon?'

'Yes, she's picked it up quickly. She's going to be a teacher just like you. Eh, Lucky? I've told her all about you.'

Lucky looked up into my face for approval and I felt afraid for her.

13

'Tell me what it's like in Scotland,' Anjali said, putting the dal on the floor and looking at me expectantly. 'Tell me what it's really like. Are there lots of women like you?'

'Like me? How like me?'

'You live by yourself, you don't have a husband and you earn your own money. And you don't care what you look like,' she added with a laugh. That stung a little but I felt my shoulders relax and got ready to laugh with her.

'Eh, Hannah!' a voice exclaimed from the doorway. I turned and saw a young man with a thick black moustache and warm friendly eyes. I couldn't for the life of me place him.

'You don't remember me, do you?' He had a deep, seductive voice and an easy, confident manner. There was a handsomeness to him that came from the way he faced you, squarely and honestly. He shook off his sandals and came in. 'Tell her who I am,' he said to Lucky but she seemed struck dumb by him. The only person unmoved was Anjali. She stood up and took the dal into the kitchen as if he wasn't there. He sat down on the bed beside me.

'I'm Anukal. Don't you remember? Gopal's boy. You used to come over to play when you weren't much older than Lucky. We rode on your tricycle. Remember that big old thing and how we all climbed on it? We used to fight for turns. You remember that tricycle, don't you?' he called into the kitchen. He seemed quite at home here. But Anjali didn't reply.

Gopal's boy. Gopal was one of the compound gardeners, a thin, obsequious little man, stooped in false humility. And he produced a son like this? Surely I would have noticed him when I was in my teens. Where had he been? Where had I been?

'How are you?' I asked.

'I'm fine. You've changed,' he said, running his hand over his head and laughing. For the first time, I felt quite pleased with my haircut.   But then Shani arrived and far from joining in the adulation, she looked at him coldly. 'I think you should go,' she said.

He accepted this meekly and sneaked me a little smile of complicity as he left.

'Mummy's waiting for you,' Shani said, smiling at me fondly. 'She's so happy now that you're here at last. Go on. She's waiting.'

'Come back again and we'll walk by the river,' Anjali said, coming out of the kitchen. She and her mother stood by their door with wee Lucky at their feet, and they waved me goodbye.

I wanted to stop and sit a while on the cement bench outside our gate where steps led down to the river. A bunyan tree hung over it, its leaves twirling in the breeze. It was a musing kind of place, with the river's strength and quietness, and the feeling of home at your back. A man was squatting on the bench, looking out over the river but when he became aware of me he turned and stared at me instead. I'd come another day, there was plenty of time.

3

THE NEXT MORNING I paused at the front door and called, 'I'm just going out for a minute, Mum.'

'Where are you going?' she said from the kitchen.

Dad was at his first class and Mum was going over with Roshan what we'd eat today and how much money she needed to give him for the shopping. He was the only one who had touched me when I arrived. Everyone else had put their hands together and said Namaskar and it seemed so inadequate after such a long time. 'Eh, Johnny Walker!' he had said, shaking my hand, his little tight, dark, angry face smiling. He always said this and it wasn't until I was about fifteen that I realised Johnny Walker was a whisky. He watched me now from the kitchen to see where I was going.

'To get cigarettes.'

'I wish you wouldn't smoke,' Mum said.

'I won't be long.'

I went down the dusty, shady road between the two compounds that led to Mahendra road. A bright blue little jewel of a kingfisher was perched on the edge of the open drain, its head cocked as it studied the grey sludge. There was food in there? I paused to watch it. Then I changed my mind; I didn't want to see what it saw. It was a quiet lane, people didn't use it much and you could hear voices of lecturers droning on from the block of classrooms. Sometimes you'd get a whiff of sulphur from the chemistry labs.

Thank God I'd finished with all that. What an awful feeling that was, coming into a classroom and those kids not wanting to learn anything from you, the ones sitting in the front with their heads ducked so you only caught glimpses of their nasty grins and those at the back tipping their chairs and chewing-gum, out to get you and you having to force your will on them every time. There were good classes and good kids but I began to realise that even though I hated the bad ones, the good ones bored me rigid. The teachers were nice but there was something so ordinary about them. You say the word teacher to people and you see them instantly classifying you – worthy, hard working, necessary, a bit dull. I did it myself. I had visions of my gravestone with the word 'Teacher' on it, and I had to get away from it.

By the back gate of the main compound several rickshaw men sat in their rickshaws, waiting lethargically for fares. One of them turned his head towards me.

'Rickshaw, Memsahib?'

'No,' I said, apologetically.

The soles of their feet were grey and hard, like cracked stones.

I turned left onto a street of shops, houses and a mosque, outside of which bearded old men in skull caps squatted under a tree. Women looked down from the flat roofs of their houses, peering over the tops of red geraniums growing brightly in rusty tins. Their teeth shone in their brown faces. 'Pagli!' a child shrieked, grinning. Mad woman. Her own head was shorn, probably because of lice. On a narrow verandah at street level two men squatted, one shaving the other. The shaver paused with his razor to watch me and the other turned his lathered face.

This road led to a bigger one where the bells of rickshaws and bicycles rang out, the wooden wheels of bullock carts bumped in and out of holes in the road, and lorries occasionally roared by. I crossed the road to a stall where a man squatted in front of a little pile of cigarettes. The stall was raised up to waist height above the drain and the man's eyes avoided mine as I wondered what kind to buy. Indian women don't smoke. There was a group of young men in tight white trousers and bright shirts hanging around the stall and they stopped their laughing and joking to watch me. The only person not looking at me was the stall holder; he was looking at his feet and wondering why I'd singled him out to embarrass him like this. An orange packet caught my eye.

'Charminar,' I said. 'One packet.'

He reached behind him and picked out a packet and placed it on the very edge of the stall.

'How much?'

'One rupee.'

That was cheap. There were only ten in the packet which meant making this journey every day.

'Two packets,' I said.

He reached behind him again and flicked the second packet beside the first. I took out my purse and handed him two rupee notes which he accepted, still not looking at me, and placed them underneath a cloth by his bare feet.

'Thank you,' I said and gave him a little smile, placatingly. I wanted more from him than this exchange of goods and money. He turned away and straightened out a pile of cigarettes behind him. The young men grinned at one another, exchanging looks.

The rickshaw men hadn't moved. They glanced at the orange packets in my hand.

'She's been to buy cigarettes,' one of them said.

'You smoke cigarettes?' another one asked.

'Yes, I do,' I replied, smiling.

'Aree,' he said, shaking his head sideways and smiling. Well, well.

I walked back down the tree-shaded lane, feeling suddenly quite happy. So you smoke? Yes, I smoke. Well, well. The kingfisher had gone, but in the shallows of the river beside the enormous outflow pipe a heron stood on one leg. It slowly brought the other leg down and took a fastidious step forward, its long beak quite still.

I ran upstairs to Mum.

18

'I'm on the back verandah,' she called when she heard me. 'I saw you coming down the lane. You were smiling. Want some coffee?'

'Yes, please.'

I sat down on one of the wicker chairs and Roshan pushed open the netted door and placed the tray of coffee on the table. He looked at the orange packet on the table and wrinkled his nose in disgust.

'Charminar,' he said. 'Very cheap. You shouldn't smoke those, they're only for rickshaw men and sweepers. Smoke Wills, they're much nicer, much better.'

'OK, I'll get those next time.'

'I wish you wouldn't smoke,' Mum said, and Roshan laughed as he returned to the kitchen. It was my health she was worried about, not my morals.

The door-bell rang and Roshan walked along the corridor in his bare feet to answer it.

'I bet that's someone to see you,' Mum said. 'They all want to see how you've turned out.'

It was Mr Biswas. He burst onto the verandah, small and loud and cheerful.

'Hello!' he cried as if greeting us at a railway station.

'Hello!' Mum said. 'Come in, come in. This is my daughter, Hannah.'

'Oh, yes.' He glanced at me for a second.

'You remember Mr Biswas, don't you, Hannah? He teaches Bengali literature.'

I did remember him, not for the literature but because he was a Marxist. I remembered him explaining to me with no irony at all that he belonged to the Kshastryia caste, the warrior caste, sitting up a little straighter as he said this. Hinduism's like that. It has room for everybody.

Today he accepted coffee and biscuits and ate and drank with vivacity, enjoying his own self-importance. His eyes, behind his black horn-rimmed glasses, darted everywhere except at me. He was full of what he had to do for his sister's wedding and the special fish he had to buy for it.

19

'This fish is very important to us Bengalis. We love it very much and it is hard to find. My parents are dead, you see, Mrs Walker, so I am the one who must marry my sisters. This means I shall not be able to marry. All the money goes on them. But –.' He shrugged and took another mouthful of coffee, enjoying the attention. 'This is our custom.' He smiled at Mum cheerily and then the door bell rang.

Roshan came to the verandah again, this time with the chief clerk of the college, Sunil Gupta. He was carrying some papers in his hand and kept his eyes firmly on Mum.

'The Sahib asked for these papers. He is not in?'

'No, he's got a class. If you leave them with me, I'll give them to him.'

'Oh, thank you.' He handed them over and then hesitated.

'You remember my daughter? Here is Hannah, all grown up now.'

'Of course, of course,' he said, shaking his head sideways, the way Indians do to mean yes or maybe or whatever you say. He looked at me for the first time.

'You've come back?'

'Yes. For a visit.'

'It's good to be with your Mummy and Daddy.' He hesitated again, still looking at me. 'You are not so –' He pushed out his elbows like a hen its wings. – 'bulky,' he said, himself an enormous bulky man standing shyly behind the group of chairs. His soft elderly bachelor's eyes regarded me for a further few seconds and then he left with another sideways shake of his head and a little smile.

Mr Biswas took up where Sunil Gupta left off.

'You know, Mrs Walker, your daughter is not at all what we imagine Western women to be. We think of them as being fast and immodest and wearing short skirts and being loud. But she is more like a Hindu girl, very modest and proper and just how a woman should be. Just like a good Hindu girl,' he repeated, smiling at Mum, pleased with his compliment. All because I sat quietly and listened to his blether.

'She is not married?'

20

'Not yet,' Mum said.

'Find her a husband here,' he cried, getting carried away.

'I'd like to,' Mum replied, winking at me. 'I could put an advertisment in the *Statesman* newspaper. Good-looking, fair-skinned, convent and B.A. educated. They'd snap you up. But you'd have to grow your hair first.'

He laughed.

But I thought they liked virgins, I was very tempted to say. 'No caste, though,' I said.

'Oh.' Mr Biswas waved his hand in the air. 'Plenty of fellows in Calcutta who wouldn't mind that. Then you would be near your mother. That's all as it should be.' He glanced briefly at me and then returned to the safety of Mum. 'I must go. A nice idea. Pursue it, pursue it.'

We saw him out to the front door but before we got there he darted into the sitting-room from the corridor and stood musingly in front of the large print of a Gauguin that hung on the high white wall. Two Tahitian women sat pensive and moody, one holding a flower. The painting, all oranges, blues and reds, was called 'When Will I Marry?'

'Decadent,' he said. 'Very decadent.' Then he left with a cheery wave.

Mum and I returned to the painting.

'I'd never thought of it like that,' she said. 'I just liked it for the colours.'

'Yes, me too.'

I felt Mum looking at me and so I concentrated on the picture.

'Let me find you a husband,' she said at last, playfully. 'I could get you a college professor, one of those tall, thoughtful Bengalis, and you could live in a flat in Calcutta and be so happy.'

The day was very bright outside and Jamuna called out in her shrill voice to one of her children.

'Convent-educated,' I said. 'Remember that nun who used to give us little kicks as she passed our desks? The kicking nun.'

She went on looking at me.

21

'What shall we do now?' I asked. Our eyes met and I looked back at the picture.

'Sarasati's had a wee baby. Do you want to go and see her?'

'That would be lovely. When did she have the baby?'

'About three weeks ago. Her others have died. We're hoping this one will live.'

We went through the main compound to the servants' quarters at the back gate. It was a low courtyard building; men were sitting under a tree outside it. We walked around the side of the building, behind which was a line of rooms unprotected by a courtyard, that opened on to a dusty area with a few blades of grass here and there. Children played around the doorways and women squatted in the dust, looking at us curiously as we passed. It was like wandering uninvited through their living-rooms.

'Eh, Hannah,' a voice called from the door we stopped at.

I peered into the darkness, making out a woman's shape. I went in and hesitated while my eyes adjusted to the gloom.

'Don't you remember me?'

It was Sarasati, Bheme's daughter; we used to play together. She had hardly changed, still pretty in a pert, young way, with her oval face and trusting eyes.

'I've come to see you,' I said.

Her little baby girl lay naked on a dirty white cloth on the bed. Her large, dark eyes had been lined with black khol and she stared intently at the cracked, soot laden ceiling. Even when Sarasati laid a proud and protective hand on her stomach her eyes remained absorbed and distant.

'Can I pick her up?' I asked.

'Yes, of course.'

The room was darkened all the more by the people who crowded the doorway looking in. I put a hand under the baby's head and the other under her tiny bottom and carefully lifted her up to my face. Her little weight was sweetness itself. Her smooth, naked bottom felt like a flower in my hand.

Sarasati's mother, Padma, pushed her way into the room. A gaunt, solemn woman, she stood smiling at the scene.

'She's just like my little Rajni. Do you remember, Memsahib?' Padma asked Mum. She covered the baby's head with a square, workmanly hand.

'I remember,' Mum said. She stood looking over my shoulder, admiring the baby.

'Who was that?' I asked her in English.

'Her own little baby many years ago. They brought her to us when she was ill but they had left it too late. She died in my arms.'

I suddenly felt a great urgency to put the baby down. I leaned over the bed but Mum said, 'Give her to me.' She cradled her lovingly at her breast.

'Is she feeding well?' she asked.

'We're giving her powdered milk,' Padma said. 'The girl hasn't enough milk herself. Look, we give her this.' She brought down a tin from a high shelf and showed it to Mum.

'How much do you give her?'

'Just what it says, Memsahib. Kershaw Memsahib told us how much.'

'That's good.' She gave the baby one last, loving look and laid her down on the bed. 'You must give her just the right amount – no more and no less.'

'We know that, Memsahib. No more and no less.'

'Do you boil the water?'

'Yes, we boil the water. She'll be all right.'

'Yes, she'll be fine.'

Sarasati and I smiled at each other.

'You're not married?' Sarasati asked.

'No.'

She shook her head as if to say, never mind.

When we left, we went through the back gate, past the rickshaws, shaking our heads at the drivers to say no, we don't need one, and went down the lane between the two compounds.

'Lovely wee baby,' Mum said.

'She lives in a hovel!' I said.

'I know.'

We giggled together guiltily. It was on the tip of my tongue to say, 'Mum, I'm pregnant.' I looked at her as she walked by my side, unconscious of my wildly beating heart.

4

'COULD WE TAKE A rickshaw to the bazaar?' I asked. My voice sounded breathless from my beating heart.

She stopped in the lane and looked behind her at the rickshaws. 'I'll have to get a few things from the flat first.'

'What things?'

She chewed the nail on her thumb and looked at the ground.

'I have to buy a wedding present for Baila,' she said. She was Jamuna's eldest daughter.

'Let's do that then. What are you going to buy her? I'll get her something too.'

I waited for her to reply as she bit on her thumb. She walked on. 'We'll get a few things first.'

When we got to the flat she stopped in the dim corridor.

'There's something I do now whenever I go to the bazaar.' Her face was closed up and hidden, almost guilty.

'What?'

'I feed the dogs.'

'What dogs?'

'Just some of the bazaar ones.' She turned away quickly, and went into the kitchen. Roshan was at the bazaar and she went to the bread tin and took half a loaf out and stood with it in her hand. The kitchen felt bare and empty without Roshan, as if he carried its secret spirit with him.

'It's something I do now,' she repeated, and took down a

small, rough jute bag from a hook and put the bread in it. 'I'm going to buy Baila a sari. Maybe you could get her some cloth to make a blouse with,' she said.

'We can go to the Kundan Market. Is it still there?'

She looked at me sharply. 'Of course it is.'

Sheraphuli was waiting for her at the entrance to the flats. Mum took out the loaf and tore off a small piece to give to her. She ate it quickly and looked up hopefully for more with her small eyes, her thick tail wagging. She was squat, white and dirty.

'Come on,' I said. 'Let's go.'

At the back gate we got a rickshaw and climbed on. 'G.T Road,' Mum said to the man and he swung his handlebars to the right, pulling the rickshaw to get momentum before starting to pedal.

The kids in the street saw us coming and at once started shrieking, 'Memsahib! Memsahib, ta-ta! Memsahib, ta-ta!' God, the delight in their wee faces, with their pot bellies and their dusty, ratty hair and their tattered vests and drawstring pants. Mum waved and said ta-ta back to them which made them shriek all the more, but I sat stiffly. I hated being a travelling freak show. There was one squatting over the drain, squirting a stream of yellow shit into it, waving and yelling. 'Wee thing,' Mum said gently, and gave her an extra wave.

We approached the back of the jute mill as a hooter sounded, and men and women poured out of the gate. They jostled past the rickshaw, most of them ignoring us. We were on a narrow road and the drains had been cleaned out but the piles of grey sludge had been left all along both sides. People were more concerned with not getting pushed into these piles than who was sitting in the rickshaw that was taking up so much space. The rickshaw driver, a tired old man with weak, stringy arms, got down and pulled the rickshaw through the crowds.

Once past the crowds, he climbed wearily back on and turned on to a busy wide road. He cycled with one hand squeezing the horn continuously. People made way for us slowly and unconcernedly, turning to see what was coming and then stepping out of our path.

'Is this the road to the Kundan Market? I've forgotten so much.'

'No, it isn't. One of the dogs is here.'

There was a moment of embarrassment between us. In a country where people are left to die on streets, feeding stray dogs was an extraordinary eccentricity; I felt it so myself.

She reached out and touched the back of the rickshaw man. 'Stop here, please,' she said.

We were outside the cinema, its huge billboards covered with the fat, pouting faces of the actors and actresses. There was something wilful about her, as if her dogs had to be by the tea shops where the young men hung about. She couldn't chose a quiet spot, not her.

A dog got up as she approached, recognising her. It had lost all its fur and its body was covered in sores. The tea-shop man watched her impassively and the men surrounded her, young and arrogant in their tight trousers.

'You like this dog?' one asked her in English. 'It is very ugly.'

She didn't reply but carried on feeding it the bread.

'Why do you feed this dog?' another asked. 'You are liking ugly things?'

They laughed.

Mum turned towards them and I could see that she was upset.

'You can laugh all you like, you stupid men. It's all your fault this place is like it is and we have to come here and waste our lives on you.'

Oh God. She had said the unsayable.

'British go home,' one shouted. They weren't laughing now.

'I wish I could,' she shouted back. 'I bloody well wish I could.'

'Mum! Come on. Let's go home.'

'Go home. Go home,' a man said. The tea-shop man gave

the crowd a warning growl and flicked a cloth at them. Mum pushed her way through them and got back on the rickshaw.

'Red monkey!' they called as the man pedalled away.

'Where to?' he asked over his shoulder.

'Kundan Market,' I said.

He took us to a street that ran parallel with the railway station and stopped in front of a wide archway.

'Shall I wait?' he asked as we got down.

'We may be a while,' I said.

'I'll wait,' he said, taking out a piece of cloth from the waist of his lungi and wiping his sweating face with it.

It was an indoor bazaar, selling material. There were little well-ordered lanes where men sat cross legged in front of bolts of cloth piled up high, neat and tidy.

'I was going to buy her a nylon one,' Mum said, stopping in front of one of the stalls. It was the first time she'd spoken since leaving the dog.

'Nylon, yes, Memsahib,' the man said. He got up and reached for several saris and spread them out, one on top of the other, greens, yellows, oranges, purples.

'Why nylon?' I asked, fingering the gritty, slippery cloth with distaste.

'They like nylon. They don't have to iron it and it lasts a long time. She's very dark. She won't suit these colours at all.'

'What about this yellow one?'

'No, not yellow.' But she picked up the end of the sari anyway and stood with it in her hand.

'Well, this green and orange then.'

'She's too small for such a bit pattern.'

'Here's a lovely pink one. She'd like all the silver in it.'

'Yes, she'd like that.'

The man knelt beside the unravelled mounds of colour and waited for us to come to a decision. Mum turned her head away and he reached behind him and pulled more saris down.

'Silk, Memsahib?'

'No, not silk,' I said quickly, before he could throw open more saris. I couldn't bear the thought of him having to fold them all away again. But it was no good. The silk saris were flung open, drowning the nylon ones.

'I don't know why I'm like this,' Mum said, and the man blinked at her.

'Like what?' I asked.

'So unhappy.'

'You should have told me in your letters.'

'I think I did mention it once or twice. But I didn't want you to get worried.'

I couldn't remember her mentioning anything like this. 'What did you say?'

'That I wanted to come home.'

I still didn't remember. But then I wouldn't have paid much attention to that. I had been too busy wanting to come home here.

'What does Dad say?'

She looked at the neat rows of cloth for another colour.

'Nothing really. I don't know what's wrong with me. I don't seem to be able to love any more.'

I reached under the silk and found the pink nylon and studied it. The man pulled it out and put it on top of the rest.

'Let's get this one,' I said.

'All right. Yes, I think she'll like that.' She was trying to pull herself together, to get into the spirit of things again.

The sari was folded quickly and economically as if it were a hanky, not six yards. Mum paid for it.

'What about the blouse material? Shall we get that later?' I said.

'We'd better get it now.'

We went to another stall and bought two lengths of cotton material, a white embroidery anglaise and a thin, pale pink to match the sari. We bought it quickly, not lingering as we used to do, enjoying the agony of choice.

Dad was waiting for us in the sitting-room as it was nearly lunch time.

'What have you got?' he asked.

We showed him the sari and he examined it carefully and then rubbed a piece of it between his fingers. 'Very nice,' he said. 'I think she'll like that.'

'That's what we thought,' Mum said cheerfully. 'I'll wrap it up in a bright plastic carrier bag. They like plastic,' she said to me. 'It lasts a long time.' She turned to Dad. 'Hannah bought some material for a blouse to go with it.'

I showed him the material but by now his interest had faded.

'Yes,' he said vaguely, and looked towards the kitchen where we could see Roshan making our lunch. Then he looked out of the window. 'Have you met the German or the Dutchman yet?' he asked.

'No,' I said and waited for Mum to elaborate. She had said very little about them in her letters. They were both unmarried. But she sat silently, looking at her toes in her sandals.

'I expect you will soon,' Dad said, looking at Mum.

That evening, when Mum and I were in the sitting room, she put down her knitting and went into the kitchen. Roshan, standing by the stove, ignored her. I watched, pretending to read the newspaper. She took out three bowls, filled them with bread and milk, and then walked self-consciously to the front door. She went past me through the sitting room instead of down the corridor; her chin was tilted, her face defiant and lonely.

'I'll chum you down,' I said. She waited for me at the door and I opened it.

There were three dogs at the entrance to the flats. She put the bowls down for them, patting them lovingly as she did so. Ganga drifted over, standing as she always did with the end of her sari over her head.

'They're looking so much better now, Memsahib.'

Mum looked at them. 'Yes, they're doing well.'

'What have you called them?' I asked.

'That one's Hugh,' she said, stroking a little black and white dog. 'And this one's Sheraphuli.'

'I know.'

'And this one's Samson. She lost all her fur after she had puppies.'

'Where are the puppies?'

'They're round by the back gate somewhere.'

Mum's face was tense. She stood looking at them for a moment and I could have said something then – what did you mean, Mum, that you can't love any more? – but I hesitated too long. She took my arm awkwardly as we went back upstairs and seemed happier.

5

THE NEXT MORNING I stood on the front verandah waiting for Mum and Dad. I was going to the chapel service that was held every morning before breakfast. I never used to go when I was young but I had my reasons now. In the river a woman stood waist high, turned towards the sun, her hands cupped to her face, praying. She ducked herself under, came up, and prayed again.

'Are you coming to chapel?' Mum asked from behind the netted door.

'Yes,' I said, coming into the room.

'Good,' she said, smiling. 'I want to show you off to everyone.'

'I'm sorry you don't like my hair.'

'It's growing on me,' Mum said.

'Ho ho,' Dad said.

A row of chairs stood at the back for the staff. The service was beginning as we arrived so we shuffled off our sandals at the door and crept to three vacant places at the end of the row. The chapel was a simple room built on to the back of the library. Sparrows chirred and crows called in the trees outside as a student took the service. The other students sat on the floor cross-legged, some of them rubbing their faces in a sleepy way.

There was a prayer going on so I ducked my head and looked along the row at all the bare feet, stopping at a man's pair, white, compact, and shapely. Next to them was a large, strong white pair. Curiosity overcame me and I looked up and met pale blue eyes and a red moustache. He raised his eyebrows and smiled conspiratorially at me. I quickly bowed my head.

The man taking the service was a Naga. Many of the theology students were tribal people from the hills of Assam and Nagaland and Missoram, from a range of mountains that sweep from Assam, through Burma and into Vietnam. They're more solidly built than the Indians, with flat, attractive faces and upturned eyes. Their grandfathers had been headhunters.

'Which one is Khup Lalzrom?' I whispered to Mum during the hymn. She didn't take her eyes from her hymn book but nodded pointedly at the young man taking the service. He had a sharp nose and thick, straight hair which fell over one eye. I'd figured he'd be like that, clever and disdainful.

After the short service I stood outside with Mum and Dad under the mimosa tree, its red, feathery bursts of flower quivering in the morning breeze. The students gave me interested glances as they returned to the hostel for their breakfast.

Mr Sen, the Principal approached, a big boned man with a dark, pompous face. He stretched out his arms and even though I knew this was impossible, I thought for one horrible moment that he was going to embrace me. But they were for dramatic effect and fell harmlessly back to his sides.

'The prodigal daughter,' he announced. I laughed obligingly.

His wife came and stood beside him, as fat, solid and sullen as before. She gave me a tight, unwilling smile.

The blue eyed European joined us. He was tall and lanky. 'I like your hair,' he said to me flirtatiously. This was something new. A flirting missionary. I didn't approve at all.

'This is the fashion?' Mrs Sen asked, staring at my head in disbelief.

'Yes,' I said.

'I thought you had been ill,' she said.

The blue eyed man was Karl Keislar, the German. This meant that the man who walked self-consciously past us, examining

33

the ground, was the Dutchman. Thick blonde hair hid half his face.

Mum took my arm and guided me to a shabby, middle-aged couple who were slowly approaching.

'Hello, Isabel,' the woman said. 'This must be your daughter.' She gave a little laugh.

'Yes, here's Hannah, here at last.'

'How wonderful for you, Isabel,' the woman said. She stood with her hands clasped over her stomach. 'Aren't you lovely and tall.' She turned to her husband. 'Isn't she?'

He laughed softly. His ill-fitting false teeth clicked and he looked at the tree beside me and then at me. 'Yes,' he said finally.

'It's been a long time,' the woman said to me.

'Eleven years.'

'Things will have changed.'

'Not really,' I said.

'No? I'm sure they have. You wait and see.' She laughed her brittle little laugh again.

As they walked to their flat next to the Library, I asked Mum, 'Who were they?'

'Didn't I introduce them? They're the Kershaws.'

'They're nice. Are they nice? They seem so.'

'They are, actually.'

The German walked back with us as he lived in the flat above us, and at our door he said,

'There is something I must discuss with you.' He flashed a smile all round.

'Come in,' Dad said gravely.

We paused in the sitting-room and Mum said,

'Have some tea. We're just going to have breakfast.'

'You English and your tea,' he said. 'Yes, I will have some tea.' Nobody corrected him.

We sat down and Roshan brought out an extra cup. Dad poured tea for all of us in his slow, careful way, turning it into a ceremony, as always, making us slow down and sit up straighter.

34

'It's about chickens,' Keislar said as Dad was pouring.

'Chickens,' Dad said.

'All the chickens kept by the servants in the compound. It's not allowed.'

'Isn't it?' Dad said.

'It's in the College rules. Servants are not allowed to keep animals.'

'They've always had chickens,' Mum said. 'It's extra protein for them.'

'They're such filthy, scrawny animals, carrying diseases. But not only chickens. What about these stray dogs? I worry about rabies, you know.'

He looked at Mum.

'Let's stick to the chickens,' Dad said.

'I have spoken several times to Lalu and Jamuna and the servants in the other compound. They stand there and they shake their heads like this,' and he shook his head sideways in the Indian way and with a foolish smile on his face, imitating and mocking at the same time. 'But they don't do anything. I keep going back and they say "Yes, Sahib, yes, Sahib," but what they mean is "No, Sahib, no, Sahib."'

Outside, the man who bought waste paper called out, 'Paper! Paper Wallah!' There was a pile of newspapers by the door but Mum sat quite still.

'I thought they might listen to you,' Keislar said. 'Lalu said to me yesterday, he said to come to you. He said I was a foreigner and didn't understand their ways. What is there to understand? But I said I would consult the experts.' He gave an ironic little bow towards Mum.

'They've always had chickens,' Mum said. 'And if they've always had something then why should they stop now?' She lifted up her chin as she confronted him.

He sighed. 'Yes,' he said, and smiled falsely at her with his red moustache and his pale, flat eyes.

'I'll talk to them, if you like,' Dad said.

'Thank you.'

We waited for him to go. But he looked out of the window

35

at the wide river. 'Your flat is so much brighter than mine even though I'm above you. The leaves of the trees block out the light. You get the brightness – but I have the birds.'

Then he got up and left with another bow.

When the door had closed behind him, Mum shouted, 'Who the bloody hell does he think he is? Just who the bloody hell!' Then she looked down at the table and her face closed up the way it went when she was dealing with the whole business of stray dogs, full of shame and pain. I was getting to know this face. Swearing made her anger seem helpless and feeble.

Roshan came in with a kettle to top up the tea pot and he stole a glance at Mum before returning. There was sympathy in his dark, tight face.

'It'll blow over in time. He'll forget about it,' Dad said. 'Something else will come up that will worry him.'

'India must drive Germans crazy,' I said. 'The way they love things ordered and in their place.'

Dad looked out of the screen door and a smile of satisfaction appeared on his face. 'So Lalu doesn't think we're foreigners,' he said.

'Of course we're foreigners,' Mum said angrily but Dad paid no attention.

After breakfast I went on to the front verandah to lean on the railing and smoke a cigarette. Mum came and stood beside me.

'I'm going to see Baila now to give her wedding present to her. Do you want to come? She's getting married today.'

'Is it today? Yes, I'll come.'

We walked down the stairs and out into the compound to the servants' quarters. These were next to our block of flats, a small group of tiny houses bunched together, two rooms for each family. Mum went to the door of the first one.

'Hello,' she called.

'Come in, Memsahib, come in,' Jamuna said, coming to the door with her neat shrewd face and her sharp eyes.

36

I followed Mum inside, ducking my head under the low doorway, and paused while my eyes adjusted to the dim light. Baila was sitting on the floor in a corner of the first room, quite alone, while her mother and several women were busy in the second.

'She's there,' Jamuna said, indicating the corner, and left to join the other women. Baila was wearing an old sari. The groom would bring the red wedding one with him.

'So, Baila, you're getting married today.' Mum stood looking down at the girl, and spoke gently.

'Memsahib,' Baila replied, looking at the floor. Her voice was a low, unhappy whisper.

'I remember you when you were just a little girl.'

'Memsahib.'

'And now you're getting married.'

Baila began to poke her fingers into the hard, earth-packed floor. She was a thin, ugly girl, good natured and anxious to please but today you just saw the ugliness. Her hair had been oiled and pulled tight off her face in a long plait and wound round onto the back of her small head. Her face, hands and feet had been painstakingly decorated with elaborate orange designs which emphasised the length of her thin face and her buck-toothed mouth. Indian girls are supposed to look miserable on their wedding day, and who can blame them, waiting for a strange man to come and take them away. Baila's husband-to-be was a sweeper in a jail in Midnapur, a town in Bihar, hundreds of miles from here.

'I hope you'll be very happy,' Mum continued, and I noticed with irritation that there were tears in her eyes.

Baila's fingers were still poking into the earth.

'We've brought you a present.'

'Memsahib.'

Mum bent down and laid the sari beside her and tried to kiss her face but the orange designs got in the way. She kissed her ear and took her hand and squeezed it. Baila made no response. I laid the material on top of the sari. Jamuna came into the room and thanked us for the presents.

'You'll come tonight?' she asked. 'And you too, Hannah?' she said, looking at me. 'And the Sahib? The Principal is coming. Lalu is preparing a chicken curry. You'll come, Memsahib?'

'Yes, we'll come. We'll be happy to come. Baila makes a beautiful bride.'

Jamuna looked at her daughter critically.

'She'll do. I've told her not to smile and hide her teeth and so long as she does that she'll be fine.' Then she looked at me and grinned. 'It'll be your turn next. Find her a husband, Memsahib. She's getting old. How old are you now?'

'She must find her own. That is our custom,' Mum replied, and the question of age was neatly avoided.

Baila's mother shook her head to show that she would never get used to the customs of these people and she smiled pityingly at me. I felt crushed between the two mothers.

Outside, Mum asked, 'What do you want to do today?'

'I thought I'd go and see Anjali for a while.'

Mum looked away and her eyes filled with tears.

'I'm so unhappy here,' she said.

I didn't know what to say. She sniffed and wiped her eyes. 'You go and see Anjali,' she said and turned away. I watched her go and at the doorway to the flats she turned around.

'Will you be back for lunch?' she asked. She knew perfectly well I would.

'Yes, I will.'

But I only made it as far as the main compound gate. Mum looked at me in surprise when I got back.

'Let's go out,' I said.

'Yes, let's,' she said. There was a sudden lightness to her and she jumped up from her chair. She had been reading the newspaper and it was unusual to see her sitting still in the day time.

'I've been meaning to paint the verandah chairs for ages. We can buy the paint today and you can help me chose the colours. I thought I'd paint each chair a different colour.'

'OK, let's do that,' I said.

'Shall we get a rickshaw?' she asked as we went down the road.

'Let's walk.'

So we walked through the bazaar to the Grand Trunk Road. We went down steps into a dark little shop and took the tins to the door to see the colours in the light while the man waited patiently. We got red, lilac, lime green, and couldn't decide on the fourth. We carried all the tins to the narrow doorway, pondering and moving out of the way of people coming in to the shop. A bottle green, we decided in the end.

On the way back we stopped at a narrow, crowded little grocery shop to buy coffee. The man said, 'Yes, Memsahib?' as soon as we came in even though there were people waiting before us.

'Serve these people first,' Mum said. The people, a small boy and a woman, looked at us curiously and gave their orders to the man.

We walked back through the Muslim area where women sat on rope-strung beds outside their dark little houses and where goats and chickens wandered about.

'How long is Paul Tulp here for?' I said as casually as I could. He was the Dutchman.

'For as long as he can,' Mum said. 'He was in Poona for a few years, doing his doctorate.'

'What in?'

'Comparative religions. We get a lot of people here from Poona. I don't know why they bother coming. They spend the whole time saying what an awful place Vishnapur is and how nice bloody Poona is. It makes me want to stick up for this place.' She never used to swear. I wasn't sure if I liked it or not.

'Does Tulp do that too?'

'He's not so bad. I'll ask him to tea one day, if you like.' She gave me a sideways look. 'I've sort of wondered about him but I thought I'd see how he reacted to you.'

'How do you mean?'

'Well, we'll just wait and see. I'll make a cake for him. He loves cakes.'

'I like his hair.'

'Isn't it lovely. He goes all stiff and self-conscious when you tell him. Do you remember what that Swiss man on the boat said to you?'

'"I like your hairs. How often do you wash them?"' This always made us laugh. Then she darted a quick look of regret at my head.

We passed my cigarette man and he studied his feet as we walked by.

It was a nice outing, the kind I had expected before arriving here, simple and uncomplicated where, when you go out to buy paint, that's all you do.

6

WE HEARD THE DRUMS that evening as we stood in the sitting-room.

'But what time will they have the meal?' Dad asked.

'I've no idea,' Mum said.

'You know what these things are like, they go on for ages.' Dad looked out of the window hungrily.

'I'll ask Roshan,' Mum said and turned towards the kitchen.

But he came over to us, his small, tight face amused at our dilemma, and joined our circle. With his hands behind his back, he tilted his head at the verandah door. 'These Hindus, when they dance around and make such a nuisance, it goes on and on and then maybe they'll think about food. The men will be drunk anyway.'

'So shall we eat now?' Dad asked, looking hopefully at Roshan.

'I've made a small meal, some dal cutlets and salad. That Lalu can't cook anyway.'

We waited for him to get the meal but he remained where he was, looking out of the verandah door.

'They say the boy drinks,' he said.

'At least he's got a job,' Mum said. She was looking out of the door with the same thoughtful expression on her face as Roshan's. The drums were getting louder.

'Well,' Dad said and moved towards the table.

Roshan smiled and went to the kitchen. When he had

41

gone, I leaned over to Mum and asked quietly, ashamed at having to ask,

'What's happening now?'

'He's getting our dinner,' Dad replied.

'That's the groom on his way,' Mum said. She went out on to the front verandah and I followed, looking down at all the preparations. Bunting had been up since yesterday, dull coloured pieces of cloth wound around the compound railings and the trees and bushes, but today they had been busy erecting a small awning outside Baila's house. It stood by itself, a faded turquoise roof of cloth on four poles. A square piece of ground under it had been painted with designs like those on Baila's face and hands. Children danced excitedly around the area and adults walked quickly past it, intent on preparations.

'What's that for?' I asked.

'I don't know,' she said.

With the drums getting louder, a spirit of festivity entered our flat. Dad brought out the gin and put four glasses on the table, filling them carefully with a measure of gin and then lime juice, bending down to make sure the measures were equal. He carried the fourth glass into the kitchen. When he came back we picked up our glasses and he said, 'Well, here's to weddings.' His eyes caught mine, briefly.

The drums grew louder and we left our meal half finished and leaned over the front verandah, waiting for the bridegroom. People ran about and children stood at the top of the road, looking down it. Above us we heard Krause's verandah door bang, and next to us I saw the glow of a cigarette from the Dutchman.

At last the group appeared. They were thin young men in shirts and trousers, dancing with their arms and legs flung about, crouching down, pulsating and jerking their bodies, laughing, dancing around the serious faced drummers. All their energy and excitement stayed within their group. The bride meant nothing to them. She was nowhere to be seen, and I couldn't make out in the thick mass of men who the groom was.

The drumming stopped when they came into the compound

and people roamed about. Nothing was happening. And suddenly there was Baila, a little figure in red sitting cross-legged under the canopy, her face lowered over her hands which rested in her lap in an attitude of misery. Nobody was paying her much attention.

'Shall we go?' I asked.

'We might as well,' Dad said.

We went down stairs and Bheme, grave and big-boned like Padma, his wife, met us at the bottom. He indicated that we should follow him and he led us into one of the classrooms opposite Baila's house. It was a stark, white-washed room, lit by two bare bulbs, and the tables and benches had been pushed together in long rows. People who I didn't recognise sat eating silently and diligently, concentrating on the meal before them. Bheme led us to an empty bench and a small boy put a banana leaf in front of each of us. Lalu came round with a huge dekchi and served us rice scooped out with a saucer. He smiled briefly at us and then Ganga came with a dekchi of curry and ladled out a huge mound that we were going to struggle to finish. It was a mostly silent room with occasional quiet talking, and outside I could just make out through the open door the red of Baila's sari.

The Principal arrived and stood at the doorway. There was a little murmur of excitement among the eaters and they paused with their rice covered fingers over their food. He raised his arms in a kind of blessing, a benign smile on his heavy, coarsened face. He refused any food and then left.

'I see Mrs Sen is not gracing us with her presence,' said a voice behind us.

It was Rahul Prakash. I knew him from before when he was a theology student and recently he had returned to teach. We made a space for him and he sat between me and Dad.

'So much food,' he said in a despairing voice, but he looked around for Lalu, caught his eye, and indicated that he was waiting to be served. Lalu came up and served him a tiny amount on his shiny banana leaf and then stood back with a sombre face, waiting for the young man's reaction.

'Aree,' Rahul said, pointing with his hand at the few grains of rice. His hands were small and neat and pleasingly expressive. Lalu gave him a few grains more, and people all around laughed. Rahul looked pained and Lalu's expression was severe. Suddenly Rahul stood up, lunged for the dekchi, grabbed it out of Lalu's hands and scooped a huge serving for himself. Lalu snatched the dekchi back, held it to his body protectively and ran away with it to the far corner of the room. Ganga came up with the curry, grinning with all her yellow teeth, and ladled out an enormous serving.

'He's a joker, that one,' Rahul said. 'He tries to starve me at the hostel. But I always get the better of him.'

He ate slowly and neatly, his fingers shaping out little balls of food which he picked up with the tips and pushed into his mouth with his thumb. Then he looked slyly at Mum and Dad.

'What's this?' he said, pointing with his clean hand at their forks and spoons. 'Is Jamuna providing silver service now?'

They moved their forks about self-consciously and laughed.

'We gave up trying to use our fingers years ago,' Dad said. 'After a particularly messy meal we noticed a missionary couple eating with spoons they had brought and it seemed such a good idea that we've been doing it ever since.'

'But Hannah, of course, doesn't need them,' Mum said, looking at me.

'Of course,' Rahul agreed, looking at my food. He had a sensuous, almost feminine mouth and small, bright eyes. He darted a look at me and spoke to his curry.

'We talk about you, you know, at the hostel.'

'What do you say?'

'Visit us and find out.'

'Tell me, please. What do you say?'

'I'm not telling. You come and visit.'

'Well, I might.'

He was the warden of the hostel, responsible for all the young men in it. Dad said that he fussed too much, and got caught up too easily in quarrels. He didn't have the authority

44

of an older man, but he was liked well enough. And anyway, he added, nobody else wanted the job. I felt sorry for Rahul, being judged by a man so sure of his own authority.

We managed to finish and really it was quite nice. Mum and Dad wrapped their spoons up in a napkin.

'Do we just leave?' I asked.

'Well, I think so,' Dad said, vaguely.

'But you must have been to lots of these occasions before,' I said.

'Yes, but I've never been very sure what happens now. What do you think, Isabel? Do we just leave?'

We huddled together outside the door, and Rahul disappeared into the crowd without saying goodbye. Baila sat like a statue, a few feet away from us. There was no one around to thank, so we left.

Upstairs, I went to the verandah and waited for something to happen. People milled about and poor Baila just sat there. I got tired and went to bed, and lay naked under the fan, thinking about Rahul and his neat little hands, and about the red glow of the cigarette from the next verandah. I liked the red glow in the dark. I spread my legs and imagined him with his blond hair, standing next to my bed, smoking, watching me masturbate.

Baila came to see us the next morning. She came into the flat pulling behind her a reluctant and moody young man.

'Memsahib,' she said, beaming and exultant. 'This is my husband.' She used the English word, husband.

The man hung his head and looked sulky but she was very proud of him. Mum greeted her like a long lost daughter.

'How wonderful you look,' she said with tears in her eyes. 'I know you're going to be very happy.'

'We're going today and I wanted you to see him.'

'How are you?' Mum asked the man.

He mumbled something and Baila nudged him sharply.

'I'm fine, Memsahib,' he said.

She was wearing her pink sari and it suited her very well. She addressed herself solely to Mum, even though I was standing right next to her. She was now in the ranks of the married, full of importance, and I was something she had left behind. Well, good luck to you, I thought, looking at the moody and morose young man. Enjoy this while you can.

When they left, Mum said, 'Wee Baila,' and smiled to herself. 'I remember when I got married first, I wanted to show Dad off to everyone, I felt so proud of him. A friend of my mother's sent me a card and on it she had written, "To Isabel and her proud choice." I'll never forget that.'

There should be a word to express a group of married women, like a gaggle or a herd or battalion. Yes – a battalion with Mum as general. General? She was more like an undercover agent. A Bond of married women, that was it.

7

S HE WENT TO THE front verandah and waved to Baila as she left. When she came back she said, 'I promised I'd go and have coffee with Mrs Wagner upstairs. She wants you to come as well. Would you like to? She wants to show me all her wedding china. She's very nice. A bit simple really and not very happy here. I feel sorry for her. Her husband has been causing all sorts of problems for the College.'

'What sorts of problems?'

'He's very fundamental. They're Southern Baptists and they think the College is far too liberal in its teaching.'

They lived in the top flat above Tulp. This was their first posting and they had been here for only eight months.

We rang the bell and a plump woman in a starched blue dress answered. She had thin, lank brown hair that hung loosely on her shoulders. She seemed pleased to see us.

'Come in, come in. Nice to see yah,' she said in a southern drawl. 'Charlie said he'd drop by and I'm waitin' for him. He tries to come as often as he can during the day, you know, Isabel?'

'Yes?' Mum replied, unsure what was being asked of her.

'We've had a long talk, like I was tellin' you I was goin' to do? And the upshot is that he's goin' to spend more time here with me. I don't know if it'll make things any better –.' We were standing in the sitting-room, grouped awkwardly around a low coffee table. '– But it's worth a

47

try.' She gave an abrupt little laugh and then turned to me.

'You must be Hannah,' she said, and put out her hand. I shook it, wary of this woman who could spill out her soul even before we had sat down.

'Glad to meet you at last. Your mother has told me so much about you. Call me Morag, that's my name. Sit down, sit down.'

'Morag?' I said. 'That's a Scottish name.'

'I know. My mother's mother came from Scotland. Some small town somewhere up north, I think, I'm not exactly sure. I've been tellin' your mother about it. She was askin' too. Hannah's a Jewish name,' she said.

'My husband's family took in Jewish refugees during the war,' Mum said. 'There was an old woman who lived with them for many years who he was very fond of, called Hannah. He wanted to name his daughter after her. And I liked the name too,' she added.

'Are you interested in the Jewish race?' Morag asked me.

'Well, a little, but not because of my name.'

'Why then?'

'Because they have an interesting history.'

'Is that right? I never thought of them as having a history or stuff like that. Just that they get everywhere. Even in Georgia, where I come from. You wouldn't think it but they're there too.'

'Is this all your wedding china?' Mum said, turning to look behind her at a long table on which plates and cups were set out in neat piles.

'That's all my stuff. It arrived two days ago and it's taken me all this time to unpack. It's been so excitin', I can't tell you. I had forgotten I had a lot of this stuff. All my clothes and things. Come and look.' She stood up and went over to the table and passed her hand lovingly over the plates.

'This was my wedding gift from my family. Ain't it beautiful? When I saw it all I just burst into tears.'

It was very ordinary china, white and green with a delicate gold pattern interwoven into the green. The cups were squat with fussy handles that looked ready to break at the slightest touch. She's younger than me, I thought as she picked up a cup.

'I know it may not look much to you, but I've never had such a thing in my life,' she said, almost apologetically.

'But it's beautiful, beautiful,' Mum cried. 'It really is lovely. Did any of it get broken?' I could hear a trace of insincerity it her voice but Morag opened up like a bright flower.

'Nothing,' she said. 'Not one thing. Ain't that marvellous? I had prepared myself for at least one thing to be broken and here it all is, not even a crack. Come on and I'll show you the rest.'

She led us into the bedroom. The shutters were closed and she opened them up but still the room looked gloomy. Piled up to the ceiling were crates along the length of the walls.

'They told us there weren't no toilet paper here so we brought our own,' she said, with a shy smile. 'Of course, when I went to the shops, the first thing I saw was toilet paper. But it's nice to have the soft American kind.'

I laughed. 'There's toilet paper in all these crates? How did you work out how much you'd need?'

'Only in some,' she said. 'But I've got my curtains at last. I'm having to remake them, sew them up together to fit the long windows here? I never imagined the place would look like this. We had talks by missionaries from villages, you know? And they never said nothin' about big houses. Don't you just love all the space in this place?' She addressed herself to Mum.

'They're lovely big flats,' I said. 'Lovely and cool in the heat.'

'Course, I'm used to heat, comin' from Georgia and all. Charlie and I are from Savannah and that's on the coast and so it's humid like it is here. But we was livin' in a trailer park. And look, look at this. I was so pleased, I can't tell you.' She was still speaking to Mum.

It was a round, shallow wicker basket with a patterned cushion in the bottom. I looked blankly at it.

'For your dog!' Mum said. 'That's nice. How is she?'

'She loves it. I put it under the fan and she sits in it, like she just knows how cute she looks. Sometimes I feel it ain't right to love a dog so much.'

She made a kissing sound with her pursed lips and there was the sound of claws clicking on the cement floor. A little hairy white dog looked round the door and then came up to me and sniffed my feet. Morag picked it up and squeezed it tight and then put it down again.

We returned to the sitting-room and drank coffee that was made for us in an enormous beige coloured coffeemaker. I guessed that arrived in the crates too. I began to feel sorry for this young woman who seemed totally unequipped for this place. But I knew her type. She'd build up an armour of disapproval and huddle inside it with her Baptist beliefs.

When we'd drunk our coffee Mum stood up. 'I have to go now,' she said.

I stood up too.

'But why don't you stay,' she said to me. 'Stay and talk to Morag for a while.'

Morag said, 'That would be great.' But I noticed a lack of enthusiasm in her voice.

Trapped, I sat down. Mum left with a wink of conspiracy at us, as if we were two lovers alone at last. I picked up my cup and drank the gritty dregs.

'I wanted Charlie to be here too. He said he'd come. Oh well, I guess he got held up in a meetin' or somethin',' Morag said. She poured coffee for both of us. She sniffed the milk before pouring it and then we heard Mum's animated voice in the stair and a man's laughter.

'That's my Charlie after all,' Morag said, and poured the milk. When he came through the door she said to him, 'Well, look a' here,' in an easy and unaffected way.

'Hey,' he said to her and stood before me, waiting for an introduction. Morag did it formally and we shook hands. He had on a very white shirt and a tie, the first I'd seen in Vishnapur. It suited his fair, earnest face.

Ganga came in and Morag called out to her in English, 'Bring the biscuits.' She said it in a haughty, arrogant way.

50

Ganga came over with a tin and placed it on the table without looking at me.

'Morag finds it hard here,' Charlie said to me. 'She isn't used to servants and everything.' He laughed a little. 'Me neither.' She remained serious and opened the tin and offered it to Charlie. He took one and held it while he spoke to me. 'Your Mom has been kind to her, tellin' her stories.'

'About when she first began,' Morag said.

'In a village,' I said.

'She's told you? The one when she was put in charge of the women's guild just because she was the missionary?' Morag asked.

'I don't think so.'

'They didn't put Pakistani women in charge in them days. I guess they do now. It was the hot weather and your Mom thought it would be nice to have the meetin's on the verandah as it was cool there? But then she heard later that the Pakistani women had said she had had it outside because she didn't want them in her house. She felt so ashamed. But I can't figure why she should feel ashamed. It weren't her fault.'

'It's just the way it was,' Charlie said, smiling at me.

'People can be cruel,' Morag said. She took another biscuit and held it in her lap. 'Mrs Sen wants me to take the Sunday school. I said I didn't have enough Bengali but she says they're only children and what I have is enough for that.' Still holding her biscuit, she burst into tears. 'How does she know?' she sobbed. Her breasts wobbled.

Charlie put his biscuit down and smiled at me again and went over and sat beside her on the wooden sofa. But she got up and went to the window. He followed and put his arm around her shoulder.

'She's havin' a bit of trouble settlin',' he said to me. 'This isn't a easy place.' He gave her his hankie from his pocket. She wiped her eyes and blew her nose vigorously and handed it back. He folded it around where she had blown her nose and put it in his pocket.

She came and sat down again. 'People are always tellin' me

what to do,' she said. Charlie sat on the edge of his chair and looked at me anxiously. I liked his protectiveness; I smiled and he smiled back. He had crinkly fair hair cut very short and skin that burnt easily in the sun.

Morag gave a big sigh and took a sip of her coffee. A tear trickled down her cheek. Charlie went and sat beside her again.

'Are you OK now?' he asked her.

'I'm OK,' she said and laid her head on his shoulder.

'Why did you leave me there?' I said angrily to Mum when I got back.

'So you could get to know each other. I didn't want to be in the way.'

'In the way of what?'

'She's been looking forward to you coming. She hasn't got any friends here.'

'What's that got to do with me?'

'I'm afraid I built you up as a possible friend.'

'You must have seen I'd have nothing in common with her. All that talk about the Jews. I'm glad we didn't start talking about the Blacks.'

'I thought you might try to be friends. What did you think of Charlie?'

'He's OK,' I said shortly, still feeling angry.

'I thought you might be lonely here, too.'

'I'm not in the least. Not in the least bit. What made you think that?'

'I don't know.' She gave an unnatural laugh, as if she had been caught doing something wrong.

'She seems so much older than me.'

'She's younger,' Mum said.

'Yes, I guessed that.'

'When I was her age I had you and was living in a village in Pakistan.'

'Bully for you,' I said angrily.

'At least she's trying,' she shouted and went to her bedroom and banged the door.

That afternoon there was a scream from outside the front of the flats, then shouts and yells. There was a deep, threatening growl from a dog. Mum and I ran down to see what was happening.

We pushed our way through the crowd that had gathered and in the middle of it crouched Morag, in helpless tears. She was trying to pull her little white dog out of the mouth of a large, fierce looking dog. The white dog was struggling silently but the large animal shook its head violently and the creature in its mouth went limp.

'He's killed her! He's killed her! He's killed her!' Morag screamed.

Govind, Jamuna's husband, pulled ineffectually at the large dog but everyone was afraid of it. Satisfied that its victim was dead, the dog dropped it on the ground, sniffed at it contemptuously, and walked away. The crowd parted to let it go. It belonged to Govind and was treated as a trophy, a huge, muscular beast that roamed the compound.

Charlie came running through the compound gate. He immediately picked up the dead dog and put his arm around his wife and pulled her away. 'The murderer! The murderer!' she sobbed as they walked up the stairs. Mum and I followed them but at the door to their flat, Charlie turned around and said, 'Thank you for your kindness. I'll see to her now.'

Mum and I went back outside.

'What a shame,' people said when they saw us. 'Poor thing.' But it was insincere. The servants didn't like her because she was rude to them and shouted at Ganga.

8

WE HAD A VISITOR that evening after dinner. Dad
answered the door bell and brought in Mr Basu. A
small, thin, middle-aged man, slightly stooping as he smiled,
came quietly into the sitting-room. Mum leaped up from her
chair in pleasure.

'How nice to see you. Would you like some coffee? It's still
warm. Let me pour you a cup,' she said.

'I hope I'm not disturbing you,' he said.

'Not at all,' Dad said, indicating in his formal way the chair
he should sit on.

'How are you?' Mum asked. 'It's been a long time since we've
seen you.'

I watched as Mum came to life, sparkling with pleasure. Dad
was pleased too.

'I am fine, thank you.'

'Do you remember our daughter, Hannah?' Dad said. 'She's
here for a short holiday.'

'Of course, of course,' Mr Basu said, smiling at me. I stood
up to greet him but was unsure whether I should offer my hand
or say Namaskar. He was equally unsure so we did neither.

'Mr Basu is head of the history department,' Mum said.

'Oh, yes,' I said, and added politely, 'I remember,' although
I didn't.

The man was all gentleness and smiles in shabby trousers and
shirt that were too big for him.

'Your mother has told me about you. You teach history.'

She smiled at me conspiratorially.

I hesitated. 'Yes . . .' I said doubtfully. He waited. 'I don't find it very satisfying,' I said, and watched as she bowed her head and studied her sandals.

'Why is this?' He appeared concerned.

'I don't enjoy teaching. I don't feel it's what I should be doing with my life.'

'Have you any idea what you should be doing?'

'No, I'm afraid not.'

'Don't be afraid. It's a good thing, to be questioning all the time.'

'She's given up her job,' Mum said.

'Ah,' he said. 'That is not so good.'

'That's what we think,' Dad said, folding his arms.

There was a pause.

'How is your family?' Mum asked, lifting her head up.

'They are well,' he said. Then he leaned forward in his chair and addressed Dad.

'I wonder, there is a matter I would like to discuss with you.'

'Of course,' Dad said. 'Would you like to come to my study?'

Mr Basu shook his head. 'I would like Isabel's opinion on this as well. If you don't mind,' he said to her, with an apologetic smile.

'No, of course not. Anything we can do to help.' She leaned towards him and we waited.

'I had a visitor this morning,' he said. 'From one of the Naxalite groups in Calcutta.' He paused to clear his throat self-consciously.

The Naxalites were outlawed because they murdered people, mostly from other Communist groups. They pulled people out of classrooms or off buses and knifed them in the head. But a lot of left-wing, intellectuals supported them because their aims were good, justice and land for the poor. It was true, there was something appealing about them.

'He came to ask me if I would hide the leader of his group in my home. The police are tracking him down and they are close to finding him.' He placed his elbows on the arms of his chair and entwined his bony fingers. 'If he is found, he will be killed.'

'Quite,' Dad said.

'Vishnapur is mostly Mrs Gandhi's Congress Party, few Naxalites. This is why they want me to hide him, they say it is safe.' He looked at his hands, still entwined; his knuckles were creased and knobbly. 'But there is my wife and my daughter. And also in my home is my younger brother and his wife and two small children. There is so much danger for them if the police find him with us.'

'Your servant,' Mum said. 'She may speak to people in the bazaar.'

'Exactly. She will be buying extra food and people will want to know who is staying with us. People are so curious, I don't know if you find this.'

'Yes, yes,' Mum said.

'Is it generally known that you're a Naxalite supporter?' Dad asked.

'Of course.'

'It's funny you should come to me now with this,' Dad said. 'Paul Tulp was talking to me the other day about his father. During the war a Jewish man asked him if he would hide him and his family from the Germans. Tulp's father had to say no because of the risk to his own family but he regretted it for the rest of his life.'

'He would have regretted it more if he had done and the Germans had found them,' Mum said.

'But he didn't know if that would have happened. It was a risk –'

'So you think I should,' Mr Basu said.

'That depends,' Dad said.

'On what?'

'On how committed you are to the Naxalites.'

'We talk about Gandhi and ahimsa and non-violence and all that,' he said. 'But in my opinion he was an abberation, almost

56

a freak. India is a violent country where life is cheap. It's very cheapness is a violence in itself.'

'Oh, I agree,' Mum said. 'I –.'

'Let him continue,' Dad said.

Mr Basu looked unhappily at the floor. 'I am always trying to justify the killings.'

Mum looked at him with her eyes round and earnest, leaning forward. Dad was sitting up straight with his legs crossed and his fingers on his lips, cool and attentive. He took his fingers away from his lips.

'When do you have to decide?'

'By tomorrow morning. But even if I say no, there is still danger. You don't say no to the Naxalites.'

'What does your wife say?' Mum asked.

'That doesn't matter now,' Dad said, irritably.

'Well, of course it matters,' she said.

'How? How does it matter? He has to decide very quickly and bringing other people into it doesn't help.'

'She's not other people. She lives there too and they must have talked –'.

'We have a very serious decision to make.'

'I know that.'

'Don't interrupt,' he said to her angrily.

'Don't speak to me like that,' Mum said, with a small, frightened anger.

He looked at her, full of a cold fury.

'I shouldn't burden you like this. I'm sorry.' Mr Basu stood up.

'Please don't go.' Mum stood up too. 'Please sit down. David will think of something. We feel very strongly for you, very much indeed. Don't we, David?'

Mr Basu sat down on the edge of his chair and Mum sat down too.

'We have to think about this slowly and carefully,' Dad said. 'Now, as I see it, you have two alternatives. One is to allow the man to shelter in your house. But then you run the risk of arrest for yourself and your family. The other is that you say no to him and then you risk reprisals from the Naxalites. Is that right?'

I could see Mum shifting with impatience.

'That is so,' Mr Basu replied.

'Then you have to decide which is the least dangerous. It seems to me that your greatest danger comes from the Naxalites. Would you agree?'

'Perhaps. Yes. Yes, that it true.' But he seemed doubtful.

'You have to be clear about this. Will they or will they not seek revenge if you turn the man down?'

'I think they will.'

'Come and stay with us,' Mum said. Mr Basu inclined his head to her but Dad ignored her. He had clearly heard her as his eyes flickered for a moment, distracted from his line of thought.

'So there is less risk if you shelter him.'

'Or if not with us, then in a flat in the compound. We have gatekeepers and night watchmen,' Mum persisted. Dad put his forefingers to his lips again and stared at the floor.

'You would be much safer here than in the bazaar. There is an empty flat in the students' hostel,' Mum said.

'What do you think?' Dad asked.

Mr Basu looked from one to the other. 'About what?'

'About bringing your family into the compound for a few weeks or a month, until this has blown over,' Dad said.

His face suddenly cleared of strain. 'Yes, yes. Yes, that is a solution.'

'We'll have to ask the Principal, but I don't see any difficulty. I'm sure he'll agree.'

There was a pause while we adjusted to the sudden way we had arrived at dealing with the problem. Mr Basu wiped his face with his hand and stifled a yawn.

'We had better go now,' Dad said, standing up.

Mr Basu stood up too. 'Thank you so much,' he said to Dad. He turned to Mum. 'Thank you for everything,' he said to her. There were tears in his eyes.

'It's so little –,' she said. Her own eyes were red.

'So little? You have saved our lives.'

58

'No, no, it's nothing. I wish we could do more. Shall I come with you and help you to move?'

'I'm sure they can manage that on their own,' Dad said, going to the front door and opening it.

'We have very little . . . . It won't take long,' Mr Basu said to her. Goodbye, goodbye.'

'Goodbye,' I said.

'Teaching is good,' he said. 'Teaching is very fine.'

'That's what I say,' Mum said.

They left. 'I'll come and see you tomorrow,' Mum called down the stairs.

The flat seemed very quiet. Mum returned to her chair and I sat down reluctantly on mine. I wanted to be doing something, not just sitting.

Mum sat with her elbows on her knees, hugging her arms and staring at the carpet.

'Poor man,' she said. 'Poor, poor man.' Her face was all suffering and her eyes drawn inward as if it were she who had to make the choice and then live with it.

'I guess nice men don't change the world,' I said. 'That's the trouble with teachers – they're so nice, and useless.'

Mum was silent.

'All his talk of injustice and life being cheap in India, and what does he do, but cheapen it himself?' I carried on.

'How? How does he do that?' she cried angrily. 'He's a very fine man.'

'He doesn't put his beliefs into practice though, does he?'

'I should have stayed with you in Scotland. It's all my fault.' She said this with deep sorrow.

'What's all your fault?'

'That you're the way you are – restless and unhappy and unsettled. If I'd stayed . . . .'

'We're talking about Mr Basu.'

'I know what we're talking about.' She looked up at me from her chair. 'You've lived a very sheltered life here. I know you were eighteen when you went back but you were very young and now you still . . . .'

'What? I still what?'

'You don't understand things.' She sighed at the floor.

I wanted to smash her face into it. 'You wouldn't have made any difference.'

She stiffened, then stood up. 'I'm going out.' She walked past me, her eyes red, and slammed the door behind her. I watched from the verandah as she went through the compound gate with a determined straightness to her back, turned the corner and disappeared.

Dad returned an hour later.

'Where's Mum?' he asked.

'She went out. I thought she was going to see you.'

'No, we didn't see her. That's very strange. She didn't say anything?'

'No, nothing.'

He looked at me as if waiting for an explanation.

'I wonder where she is,' he said.

'Did you sort everything out?'

'Yes. He's moving in to the flat tonight. The Principal wasn't very happy about it but I persuaded him. He's been doing his best to keep the police out of the compound and this kind of thing risks bringing them in.'

'Will he be all right?'

'Yes, I think so.'

'Really? I wouldn't have thought a compound wall would keep them out.'

'It's surprising, you know.'

'Yes, I suppose so.'

There was a pause as we stood in the middle of the sitting-room. I picked at a hole in the material of Dad's chair.

'She just went out? Not saying a thing?' he asked.

'That's right.'

He looked at the front door. 'A funny thing to do.'

The hole gave a little and I smoothed the tear down.

'Well, it's getting rather late. I think I'll go to bed,' he said.

'Yes, it is late.'

'What are you going to do?'

'I'll go to bed as well.'

'Goodnight, then.'

'Goodnight.'

I went to my bedroom, undressed, and lay in bed. I heard Dad in the bathroom, and then in the bedroom, and in the silence I knew that he was saying his prayers, kneeling beside his bed, his hands covering his face, as he did every night. When I was small I came into their bedroom one night and discovered them praying; Mum was kneeling by her bed with her face hidden too. She got up quickly and ushered me out but he didn't move.

I tried to imagine what his prayers sounded like. 'Dear Jesus.' No. I had said that as a child when I said my prayers with Mum. Dear. That was how you began a letter. 'Lord God.' When he prayed from the pulpit in church his prayers began, 'Dear Lord.' They were sincere prayers that addressed a listening God. He asked for help in overcoming doubt. He stood up straight with his eyes closed and his head bowed, holding on to the pulpit as he acknowledged weakness and prayed for strength. He always seemed sure of everything but underneath it all there had to be in him, as in everyone else, doubt and weakness. But he asked for help with such simplicity as to make doubting seem a strength.

'Lord God.' But it was no good. I couldn't imagine his prayers, but I could have said Mum's for her. 'Dear God, forgive me, forgive me.'

At last the front door opened and Mum was back. I heard their quiet, muffled voices and then there was silence, and the last thing I heard before I went to sleep was a dog barking from somewhere in the bazaar.

9

WE WERE LIGHT AND friendly with one another for a few days as if nothing had happened, but she went out a number of times without saying where she was going and I guessed she was visiting the Basus. She always came back cheerful from them.

'There's a beautiful baby competition this afternoon,' she said on her return from one of these visits.

'They have those here?' I asked.

'I've said that you'd be a judge in it.'

'Oh, no. You didn't, did you? Are you joking?' I said.

'No, I'm not joking. It's not a joke. I'll make coffee and tell you all about it. Dad should be back soon from his class.'

We went into the dark, hot kitchen, emptied of Roshan's presence.

'But why did you do that?'

'I promised I'd do it, but I've got to meet Kaliya this afternoon about painting the married students' quarters, and when I said to Mrs Mitra that you'd come instead of me, she was very pleased.'

I doubted that. 'Mrs Mitra,' I groaned.

'I don't know why you're making such a fuss.'

I clattered cups onto the tray and then looked in drawers for teaspoons.

'If you feel that way, I'll go and tell Mrs Mitra that you can't do it,' she said.

'No, I'll do it. Since you promised,' I said, sulkily.

Dad returned and we went on to the back verandah, Mum carrying the coffee and cups on a tray.

'Mum has volunteered me to judge a beautiful baby competition,' I said to him, expecting him to take my side.

'It'll give you something to do,' he replied.

'It's at two o'clock,' Mum said. 'In the hall above the library. Mrs Mitra will tell you what to do.' She was upset now. Her cheerfulness had the fragility of cracked glass.

'Mrs Mitra?' Dad said. 'I'm surprised she's doing it.'

'So am I.'

'Why?' I asked.

'Her daughter's wee baby died in the night a few weeks ago. They say there was no reason for it, but we think she must have lain on the baby in her sleep and suffocated it. It's quite common here,' Mum said.

'Is it?'

'Yes, it is.' Her elbows were on the arms of her chair and she was bent over her hands, playing with her rings, unsmiling, closed into this mood that had swooped down from nowhere.

'You'll probably enjoy it,' Dad said, his mouth full of biscuit.

There was a pause, and then suddenly half a dozen golden oriels flew around the trees in the garden.

'Oh, look!' I cried and Mum raised her head. We watched the yellow birds glistening in the sunlight. They swooped around for a second time, flying parallel to the verandah.

'I've never seen that before,' Mum said.

Then Dad said, brushing crumbs off his trousers, 'We were wondering, Hannah, what ideas you've had for work.'

'Nothing, really.'

'You must have given it some thought.'

'Yes,' I said, smiling at him.

'What have you thought?' He looked at me steadily.

'That there isn't anything I want to do.'

'Have you crossed off certain things?' Mum asked, softer than Dad.

'Yes, I've crossed a lot of things off.'

'What are they?' he demanded.

'What would you like to do in your heart? What is it you dream about?' Mum asked.

'Her dreams won't pay the rent or get her anywhere.' He turned his severity on Mum now. His grey eyes were cold and he leaned towards her almost threateningly. 'It's not dreams you want to encourage, it's hard practicalities.'

I knew that if I gave a little of myself they would be satisfied. If I opened the door to my heart just a crack it would be enough for them. But there was the risk that Mum would wrench it open and grope about greedily. She took hold of my arm.

'How about social work?' Dad said.

'No.'

'Or advertising.'

'No.'

'Or publishing.'

'No.'

'Working for an international charity, like Oxfam.'

'No.'

'Well, what are you going to do?'

'I don't know,' I said quietly.

'Let her tell us what she's been thinking about. She must have some idea,' Mum said.

They looked at me and I looked back at them.

'No, I haven't,' I said.

Mum still had her hand on my arm. 'Maybe we're thinking along the wrong tracks. How about hairdressing?'

I bent my head and shielded my eyes with my hand and began to cry. Mum tried to pull my hand away.

'I don't want you to drift and have no money and be unhappy. You've led a very sheltered life both here and in Scotland, but you've got to go out and push yourself and fight for yourself.' She held on to the hand that was covering my eyes.

'Well, perhaps we'd better leave it for now,' Dad said. I heard him push his chair back and stand up. 'We didn't mean to upset you. As Mum says, we wanted to be sure you were thinking about the future.'

'I am.'

'That's good.'

'But what are you thinking? Don't go away, David. We haven't come to any conclusions. She doesn't know what she wants.'

'We can do that another time.'

I heard him walk away and then his study door closed quietly and Mum sighed. She took her hand away from mine and began to twirl the rings on her fingers again.

'I wanted to be a dancer, you know.'

'Did you?' I wiped my nose with the back of my hand.

'I probably wouldn't have been very good.'

'Probably.'

'Och, well,' she said, sitting back in her chair.

The ugliest baby won. It had pale skin, rolls of fat, and a wet, sulky mouth.

The competition was outside the library, under the trees in front of the steps. Tables had been brought out and the babies sat on the tables or were held by their mothers, watched by an audience of curious students, relatives and compound servants. The servants stood in the background and some of them waved to me as I walked around the tables with Mrs Mitra.

There was a thin, dark baby with enormous, solemn eyes sitting naked on the table. It had a tiny, glittery bracelet on each wrist and I shyly touched its little pink palm. It looked down at the place that I had touched and then up at me, its expression never changing. Mrs Mitra hustled me away.

'Not that one,' she whispered loudly. 'Here, here. Oh, there are so many. What shall we chose?' She laughed joylessly, touring the tables laden down with babies, ignoring the anxious mothers, bustling about, bending down to inspect, her mouth a thin, straight line in her small, fat face, while I followed, smiling apologetically at the mothers and hating the whole business.

She stopped for the second time in front of the fat, pale baby. 'This one. Don't you think? Yes, this one.' I thought about objecting, but didn't want to draw out the affair any longer.

She seemed as relieved as I was that the choosing was over. She picked up the baby, gave its cheek a squeeze which made it cry, and then handed it back to its mother.

'It's so well fed,' she said. 'That is the main thing. Some of these other ones – they must feed them on milk and water just. Don't you think?'

'They're all lovely,' I said.

'Yes, yes, of course. They are all so lovely. Tell Mummy I'll come and see her soon. You've been such a help. Mummy must be so pleased to have you back.'

That little pink palm had upset me too much to see Mum. I passed Anjali's house and saw that the door was open, so stepped in to the netted verandah and called, 'Are you there?' as I used to as a child.

Anjali was sitting on the floor, with Shani and Roshan standing over her. The anger on their faces turned to embarrassment when they saw me.

'Come in,' Shani said, without enthusiasm.

'I'll come back later.' I looked at Anjali who avoided my eyes.

'No, no. Come in now. I'll make some tea.' Shani was in her petticoat and as she stood up I caught a glimpse of her brown legs through a tear. She laughed shrilly, clutching at her torn petticoat.

'Sit down,' Roshan said, indicating the bed, and I sat, trapped by their reluctant hospitality.

Shani called from the kitchen, 'Bring me my sari.' Anjali got up and took it through to her; she came back and sat on the floor again. There was an awkward silence until Shani came back.

'I've been judging beautiful babies. The ugliest baby won.'

They looked at me suspiciously.

'Mrs Mitra chose it. Have you ever entered Lucky in it?'

'No. She's too ugly. Too black, like her father.'

Shani loudly drew in her breath. 'The trouble with babies is that they grow up,' she said, looking at her daughter. 'Eh? They grow up. Maya dies in childbirth, Amit gets a girl pregnant, Vijay goes off to the navy and God knows where he is, he never writes,

66

he might be dead for all I know. And then you – of all my babies you were the one I thought I could rely on.' Shani, thin and tough, looked at her daughter with dry, angry eyes.

'We marry you to a good man and you get a chance to go and live in the South – to go home. My God, what I'd do to be able to go home.'

The dekchi full of water bubbled and hissed over the fire, but no one paid it any attention.

They were Catholic Madrasis who spoke Tamil to one another and Shani had taught them to write in a script that looked like unravelled knitting. Although Shani spoke so longingly of home, she and Roshan both came from families who had lived in Burma. Many Indians had gone there. When the war came they had fled from the Japanese; they met on that terrible road to India, both the only survivors of their families. Everyone else had been killed by Japanese bombs. Even now, Roshan didn't like the Naga students with their slanting eyes and flat faces.

'He was the wrong man,' Anjali said quietly.

'Wrong man, right man, what does the man matter. Eh? He gave you a home, he gave you a daughter. Did he beat you? Well, did he?'

'You know he didn't.'

Anjali sat with her chin resting on her knee, her other leg curled under her.

'Did he have other women?'

'I don't care about other women.'

'We've been through all this,' Roshan said. He gave Anjali a soft and loving look, which surprised me. If anyone was going to be angry I would have expected it to be him.

'You're neither married nor unmarried,' Shani said. 'You've got no money, no life of your own. What'll you do when we die?'

'Are you putting me out?' Anjali asked. 'Are you forcing me to go? Are you throwing me and Lucky out of this house?'

'I will if I have to,' Shani said.

'No, we're not going to do that,' Roshan said. 'We'll never do that. For God's sake. Eh, Johnnie Walker.' He sighed loudly, coughed, and went to the door and spat, projecting the globule of phlegm into the grass beyond their yard.

Anjali stood up. 'You should have let me marry Anukal.'

Shani stood up too. Her eyes shone with fury as she came towards her daughter. Anjali stood still, cowering slightly.

'Marry a Hindu,' Shani said, her voice low. 'You don't understand anything, anything at all. What have you got in your head – mud from the river? Eh? Eh? Where do you think you're living? Scotland? That's it, isn't it? You think you're living in Scotland, like Hannah, and can do as you like. Ask her if everything's so wonderful there. Go on, ask her.'

I opened my mouth to tell them that no, it wasn't so wonderful, but Shani didn't wait.

'You're not there, you're here and we've got to sort you out and get you back to your husband. Isn't that so?' she said to Roshan. He was looking moodily out of the door at the baby competition tables being dismantled. He grunted in reply.

Anjali walked out of the door, brushing past her father. I followed, glancing apologetically at Shani.

We walked in silence for a while. Then Anjali said, 'I'm going to the waterworks. I always go there after a quarrel.'

'You've had this fight before?'

'Lots of times. She can shout as much as she likes, I'm not going back to him.'

She drew the end of her sari over her head to hide her tears. There was an unexpected stubbornness to her now. She used to be a timid, hesitant girl, wanting to please, never going against authority.

'I didn't know you wanted to marry Anukal,' I said. She was shy and quiet, not a pretty woman with her long face and her small, self-doubting mouth. He would have been quite a catch, I thought enviously.

She looked out over the brown, wide river. 'He said he'd convert, but they wouldn't listen. It's because he's a sweeper's son.'

'But he's a technician in the science labs,' I said. 'He's done very well.'

'He doesn't have any caste,' she said irritably.

'Oh.'

She wiped her eyes with her sari. 'They went down South and found a husband for me in a hurry. Anukal's family brought a girl over from his village for him to marry, a jungly, stupid girl who can't even read and write.'

'What's your husband like?'

Anjali didn't reply. She wiped her nose with the back of her hand and the question hung between us. We reached the broken-down gates of the waterworks and passed the house of the gatekeeper who watched us warily but let us through.

The waterworks was a wide, open, green space on the banks of the river. There were several water tanks, surprisingly clean with pebbles and sand at the bottom. She led the way to a ruined Hindu temple, the foundations of which the river was slowly washing away. It was a heavy, round building, open to the air and the river, a series of high, thick arches, graceful in its ruin. We sat down amongst the sand and stones on the floor.

'He's a fisherman and he's quite rich,' she said. 'He owns two boats. He's always working and when he comes home he's tired all the time. He's an old man.' She threw a stone onto the muddy bank. 'My mother expects me to be grateful for all of that. She talks on and on about the sea and the South and home but she's never lived there. Her mother was the one who left it all behind to go to Burma and she used to talk about the fishing boats and the nets drying in the sun and now I'm the one who has to live there.'

I liked the sound of it. It didn't seem such a terrible idea, setting up home in a place like that.

We sat in silence for a while. 'How is Lucky?' I said in the end.

'She's fine. She's at her tutor's now.'

'Oh. How's she doing?'

'Fine.' She was drawing patterns in the sand.

'I suppose it gives you a bit of time to yourself while she's away.'

'I get on with my work.'

69

'Work?'

'Preparing the meals, cleaning, that sort of thing.'

'Oh.'

She drew little circles.

Finally, she said, 'I have to get back for Lucky now.'

We stood up, brushed the sand off our clothes and walked back home. On the way, we had to pull over to the side of the road as a funeral procession approached. The dead person was bound in a sheet and was carried on a rope-strung bed on the shoulders of four men. The bed bounced slightly to the rhythm of their walk, the tightly bound head bobbing up and down. The men's faces were solemn and absorbed, poor-looking men in lungis and shirts, like rickshaw drivers.

'I wonder who it was,' I said, and she shrugged.

10

'Let's go to calcutta today,' Mum said to me enthusiastically at breakfast. 'It's about time we had a day out.'

'OK.' But I was wary of Mum's cheery moods that cracked apart so suddenly.

We finished breakfast in a hurry to catch the 8.30 Vishnapur Local.

The station was crowded with people going to work but there was no bustle, only a quiet anticipation of the train. This was one of the few that started from Vishnapur and so arrived empty. The rest pulled in crammed with people. Waiting for the busy trains was like anticipating the surge of battle. People bulged out of the carriages, hanging on to the pole in the centre of the wide doorway. My heart used to tighten with fear all those years ago. Mum loved this battle. She was in her element, waiting with her chin up and her eyes alert. She said to me once, You should have more of the tiger in you, Hannah.

The train rattled in. There was only a small rush for seats and I got one next to the barred window and Mum sat opposite me. Across the aisle a group of four men spread a thin white cloth across their knees and began a game of cards. People standing nearby watched the game.

'I'll make a list of everything we've got to do today,' Mum said. She got out her notebook and the man sitting next to her looked over her shoulder with interest.

The train filled up from station to station, town to town.

71

People fought and struggled to get on, running from carriage to carriage, some giving up in despair. I can get on your trains and you can't, I thought smugly. Between the towns were fields, patches of rural life and thatched huts amidst the factories. Black buffalos were led along the edges of green rice fields to the water tanks where women washed clothes.

'Do you want to read the newspaper?' Mum asked.

'No, thanks.'

An old blind man pushed his way through the crowded carriage, his hand on a wee boy's shoulder. The boy stopped at each group of seats and silently held out his hand while the man asked for money. Mum put her notebook down, took out her purse, got money out and reached towards the child. Her neighbour took the money from her and put it into the boy's hand.

'Thank you,' she said to him.

He bowed his head slightly to her.

We approached Howrah station and the railway lines spread out and became tangled. We passed commuter trains, equally crowded, clicked over uneven points, passed steam engines and diesel engines, empty trains in sidings, postal trains, railway workers, line mending engines, abandoned carriages. We came in to the terminus with the slow rhythmic clicking of wheels on rails, and a final screech of brakes.

Mum folded up her paper and left it on the seat. We squeezed out with the crowd, and when we were walking down the platform, her neighbour on the train tapped her on the shoulder and said, in English,

'You left your newspaper.'

'Thank you,' Mum said, taking it. 'That's very kind of you.'

He bowed slightly.

'Now what am I going to do with it?' she said when the man had passed us.

'You could try leaving it on the bus.'

We walked quickly through the huge Victorian station, dodging families and their luggage on the floor. The trick was to reach the buses before all the other people coming off the trains.

'Do you want to take a tram or a bus?' Mum called over her shoulder.

'I don't mind,' I said, half running to keep up with her.

'We'll get a mini bus. They're new. You don't know them.'

She led the way to the bus station where lines of buses were parked. There were red double-deckers and green minibuses. I was glad we weren't taking a double decker. I remembered the way they angled dangerously with the weight of people crammed in at the door. I'd heard that double-deckers were almost impossible to capsize. Whoever said that hadn't been to Calcutta.

Mum ran along the mini buses.

'Park Street!' she cried. 'Park Street!'

Some conductors shook their heads. Others waved her further on.

'Park Street, Memsahib!' a conductor finally called, and we climbed breathlessly into the tiny bus.

'I remember,' Mum said, laughing, as we sat down and waited for the bus to fill, 'when your uncle James came to visit us. He was living it up real swanky with posh hotels and all his drink, so I thought a minibus would be good for him. Show him, you know.' She laughed again. 'We were squashed up in the bus – it was full and we had to stand. I looked round to see how he was doing and I couldn't see him. I panicked and shouted, "Stop the bus. I've lost my friend!" Then a cross voice said, "I'm here." His back had got so sore with bending that he'd got down on his knees on the floor.'

The bus filled up and we joined the traffic crossing Howrah Bridge into Calcutta. There were bullock carts, men pulling two-wheeled carts, horses pulling tongas, buses, trams, lorries, cars, taxis, and men and women carrying loads on their heads, moving in a hip-swaying half run. On the Calcutta bank, darkened by shadow and mud, smoke rose from funeral pyres. The river glinted grey in the sun and brown in the shadow of the bridge. Tugs, barges and small boats moved about on the water. Further up, the river curved away, and was lost in a haze of heat.

Out of the bottleneck, the bus wound its way through

the traffic. The conductor leaned out of the door, shouting, 'Esplanade! Chouwringhee! Park Street!' It went up a ramp-like road into China Bazaar, and drew level with dark open windows and women on flat roof tops drying their long hair in the sun. Then down past St Andrews Church, around Dalhousie Square, with its huge water tank and the government buildings, and into the Esplanade, where the Maidan began. The huge, flat, open space of the Maidan was filled at this end with vendors and trams. A squatting man in rags licked the remains of food off banana leaves that had been thrown on to the ground.

We got off at the top of Park Street. It was a wide, nineteenth-century street, with a seductive feel of decay and past glory.

'This way,' Mum said, and stepped into the road. A car came straight for her, its horn blaring; we paused to let it pass. Cyclists weaved around us, ringing their bells. We paused for another car, and then I saw a man on the other side. Had Mum seen him? She didn't let on, but once she had aimed herself at a particular direction, there was not a lot that could stop her. This might, though. The man was naked with matted hair and a round belly, not an unusual sight in India. He could have been a sadhu or just a nutter. Indians can be amazingly tolerant of all types, but in the case of mad people, they prefer to ignore them. This one was hard to ignore. He had the most enormous erection I'd ever seen. He was leaning back against a lamp post, his eyes shut and his erection projecting across our path, like a turnstile we had to push aside.

We made a slight detour in utter silence, out Indianing the Indians in our apparent nonchalance. I felt mesmerised; I had to tear my eyes away. I gave a nervous little giggle and turned to Mum but she was looking fixedly at a shop window. Poor Mum. Floored by an erection.

'We'll go to Flury's first,' she said, still looking at the shop window. 'I want to buy you lots of cakes.'

When she was not long married, she and Dad set off for Pakistan for the first time. Her parents came to the docks at Liverpool to see them off; it was going to be five years before they saw her again and Pakistan was a long way away in those days. It was more unknown, with a sense not of when but if I see you again. That's the way she tells it, anyway. Her loving, gentle Dad bought her lots of cakes in a café. Cakes were very expensive but she was so nervous that she couldn't eat them. Her Dad died a few years later and if there was one thing she'd do again, it would be to go back and eat those cakes.

'One will do,' I said.

'Two at least,' she insisted. 'To celebrate you being here. Many's the time I've been here on my own and wished you were with me.' She took my hand and squeezed it.

I always felt uncomfortable when Mum touched me. It was as if she were reaching for a soft part of me that wasn't meant to be touched. I pulled my hand away.

'Two cakes it is then,' I said and we walked on.

11

'I'D LOVE A FLAT in Park Street,' Mum said, looking up at them. 'I think that if I could live here, I'd be happy.'

I looked up at the flats and saw into Mum's dream of uncomplicated glamour and interesting friends and maybe even handsome men.

'Wouldn't you?' Mum asked.

'I don't know.'

'I would. Dad would like to live here too. There's a flat you can see from a window at Flury's and we both decided that's the one we would like.'

They were always choosing flats or houses they'd like to live in, and I'd caught the habit from them. But it was a habit I didn't like as it reminded me of my homelessness.

'Maybe the neighbours wouldn't be nice,' I said.

'You're right. Maybe the neighbours wouldn't be nice.'

The café was nearly empty, and waiters in white uniforms gazed out of the windows. An older one tried to entice us to one of his tables in the centre of the room but Mum led us to a window seat. The shades were half drawn against the sun and fans were turning slowly in the large bright room. A young waiter came and stood by our table, his hands behind his back.

'We'll have cakes, please,' Mum said to him. 'And two coffees. Or would you like lime juice and soda? Dad always has that. You used to like it. Or both. Have both. Two coffees, please, and one lime juice and soda,' she said to the waiter, before I could say anything. He nodded his head vaguely and wandered away.

'I've got my list here,' Mum said and got it out of her bag. 'What shall we do first?' She studied it for a moment, giving it all her concentration.

'This place hasn't changed at all,' I said. 'I think even the waiters are the same. That old one there – he was here before, wasn't he?'

'I think they're all the same. The toilet's just as bad. I keep complaining but they still haven't mended it properly. You remember there was always a bucket of water by the potty because the flush never worked? It's still there. I want to take some cakes back to Dad. I promised him I would.'

'Do you remember when we bought three dozen chocolate truffles here for that meeting of the College Senate –.'

'And by the time we got them home they were all just one big mush. We had to roll them up again and cover them in icing sugar. People loved them and kept saying to me how nice they were and I thought, If only you knew.'

We laughed together and Mum said, 'It was fun then.'

Our waiter came back and put a menu on our table and went away again.

'It wasn't fun then, Mum.'

There were times, not many, when she banged around the flat, shouting that she was going to divorce Dad and leave this horrible place. Dad and I stood in silence, waiting for her to do what she always did, which was to apologise.

A group of four fat young men came in talking and laughing. The sounds from the street came in with them, car horns, rickshaw bells, voices, sparrows chirping, crows cawing. Then the door closed and the sounds became muted.

'No, it wasn't fun then,' Mum said, watching the men. 'But somehow things have got worse.'

'How? In what way?'

'I don't know.' She looked at her list. 'You know how things can go wrong.'

'Yes, I do,' I said.

Mum looked at me, as if she'd found the naked part she'd been looking for. 'When I was your age, I had a baby – you – and was living in a village in Pakistan, married to a man who worked all the time, and far away from my family. I managed – you do, somehow – and I made mistakes, but somehow I got through it. But it's very different for you now. We're in a more questioning age where people are encouraged to fulfil themselves and I suppose the freedom you have is good, but I think it makes it more difficult too.'

'It is difficult, that's true,' I said, trying to sound vague as if I were talking about other people.

'It was expected of me that I'd get married. I think my mother felt I had made a good catch. I was expected to have a baby and I did. I was expected to follow my husband to a strange country and I did. I follow him in everything. Although, it's funny, when we have to make decisions on little things he doesn't pay me much attention, but when it's on a big thing – I don't mean theology or anything like that – but on say, whether to appoint a new Dean, or what to do about the troubles with the minister of the church, then he listens very carefully to what I have to say.'

I remembered Mr Basu.

'But what I'm trying to say,' she continued, 'is that if I hadn't got married, it wouldn't have been so terrible. I was a probation officer and it was a good job and I enjoyed it very much. But then I got married . . .' She turned to look at the waiters standing about. 'I remember when he first asked me out,' she said, picking up the menu. Her face softened as she spoke. 'He was living in a boarding-house in Edinburgh where the landlady made him tea all the time and brought it up to him on a tray and cooked his meals for him and brought him up his newspaper. Old ladies have always liked him. When I'm gone, I know he'll find someone to look after him and cook for him and think he's wonderful. Don't let him get you to do that. Especially if you aren't married. Single women are expected to do that but don't waste your life looking after him.'

'When you're gone where?'

78

She put down the menu and picked up her notebook. 'When I'm dead,' she said, looking at her list.

'Oh, Mum.' I'd never thought of life without her. 'Don't say that. You've got a long way to go yet.'

'Maybe. I come from a family who drop dead at an early age.' She spoke lightly of it, as if she was instilling fear into me on purpose. 'He wrote me a letter asking if I'd like to go to the theatre with him, and we passed it all around the table, my Mum, my Dad and my brother all trying to read his handwriting so that we could figure out which theatre he wanted to meet me at.'

'Did you work it out in the end?'

'We did in the end. Otherwise I wouldn't be here now.'

She meant it as a joke, but we looked at it thoughtfully, trying to smile, but not able to.

'Hello!' a voice suddenly said. A man had sat down at the table next to ours, an elderly man with a large bulbous nose and blotchy, pale skin.

'How are you?' he asked.

'Very well, thank you,' Mum answered. 'And how are you?'

'Oh, not so bad. This damned heat, you know. How are things at home?'

Home? I wondered. I hadn't seen him in Vishnapur. Maybe he was one of the Parsee engineers from the jute mill.

'I don't really know,' Mum said. 'We get bits of news in the papers. Things seem fine.'

'Yes, indeed. The climate will be so pleasant there now. Nice and cool, what? Nice and cool.'

Mum smiled stiffly and then turned pointedly to me.

'Where's that waiter? The service here is so slow. I think he's forgotten us,' she said in a loud voice.

Then she nodded slyly towards one of the tables in the centre, where the fat young Indian men were tucking into plates of beans on toast.

'They think it's very posh,' she said, smiling. 'All the sophisticated girls from Loretto's come here in their tight jeans and high heels and they eat beans on toast too.'

'Who's the man?' I whispered.

79

She picked up the menu and pretended to study it. 'He's an Anglo-Indian,' she whispered. 'Whenever he sees me he always asks about home. I shouldn't think he's ever been there. Not from the way he talks about the place.'

The waiter arrived with our coffee and my lime juice and soda.

'And the cakes,' Mum reminded him. He gave a little nod and wandered away again. We watched as he stopped for a chat with another waiter and then he walked aimlessly to a counter and stood and waited. Finally, he produced a tray and carried it back to us. I chose a chocolate truffle.

'What about this one?' Mum said, pointing to a huge cream filled horn.

'All right,' I agreed and the waiter placed it on my plate, beside the truffle.

Mum chose a danish pastry. Now at last with our cakes, we settled into our chairs. Mum drank her coffee and studied her list again.

'I know you're having troubles and I can see that you don't want to tell me about them, and that's OK. Not everyone wants to confide in their mother. I didn't tell my mother everything.' She took a sip of coffee. 'But the thing I want to say is this. Don't feel you have to get married. You may meet the right man soon. You're still young. But if he doesn't come along that doesn't matter. I know a lot of single women who are very fine people. When you're single you can do things, you're free to do things, and these women have worked and are very happy in what they're doing. They have their work,' she said, looking earnestly at me. 'That's what is important, and that's why I was so upset when you said you had given up teaching. Maybe it's not the right thing for you, but you have to have something.'

'I'll find something, Mum. I'll be all right.'

'But what?'

I didn't reply.

'Just don't get pregnant,' Mum said. 'I often read in magazines about girls like you who are rather lonely and lost and who get pregnant and they think the babies will solve their lives, and maybe they do, but it seems an awful thing to do to a little baby.'

'What do you mean?'

'Well, babies grow up, you know.'

'Of course they do.'

'There doesn't seem to be any of course about it in the magazine articles.'

I mashed the cream with my fork.

'What else have you got on that list?' I asked, trying to joke.

She returned to it with a serious face.

'I want to get material for a dress. And then we need to go to the Newmarket for grocery things. And there's a shop there that sells ready-made clothes. I thought I'd look in that. And Dad wants me to ask in the Oxford Book Shop for a book for him.'

'What kind of ready-made clothes are you looking for?'

'Oh, I don't know. Something nice, a dress.'

'I've nearly finished.'

'Don't hurry. We've got all day. Of course, it's not very nice for the mother either,' she said.

'What isn't?' I took a bite of the cream horn and concentrated on the cream that oozed out.

'Having a baby when you're not married.'

The cream was getting everywhere.

'It's difficult enough when you are married,' she said.

'Not everyone begins as a mother in a village in Pakistan,' I said.

'That's true. But even so. Just don't.' She took a forkful of my cream and then handed me a napkin.

'Was it so awful for you?' I asked.

'No, of course not. No, no, not at all. You were a very good baby. Everybody said that. A lovely fat wee baby with podgy wee hands. You never even got sick.'

I licked my fingers slowly, one at a time. She picked up her bag and put the notebook back in it and then signalled to the waiter. He ambled over. 'The bill please,' she said. 'Let's hope there's water in the taps today.'

There wasn't. She turned on the tap but it coughed emptily. I shut the door behind us and locked it. It was a small windowless room, blue all over, walls, ceiling and floor. The potty was on a raised platform like a stage and Mum looked into the bucket beside it.

'Plenty of water there anyway,' she said. 'You go first.'

'No, no, you go. I can wait.'

'All right, if you don't mind,' she said, and stepped up onto the stage. 'I'm rather desperate.'

She pulled up her dress and pulled down her knickers as far as her knees and half-squatted over the toilet.

'You don't get VD from toilet seats, you know,' I said, watching as she peed straight down into the bowl, making a hollow filling up sound. I smelled it too. The skin on her thighs was very white.

'I know,' she said, 'but I can't help feeling that you do. My mother used to warn me.' She finished and waited until the drops had gone and then leaned down to the bucket and wet her hand and wiped herself with it and then wet her hand again. Then she hobbled off the platform and fished around in her bag with her dry hand until she found a hankie and dried between her legs.

It was my turn. I sat on the cracked plastic seat.

'When my mother was a young woman,' Mum said, standing in front of the mirror with her comb in her hand, 'she used to pee half standing but she didn't pull her knickers down, she just pulled them to one side, only because she was in a hurry and couldn't be bothered. She used to leave the door open and *her* mother used to say, "One day someone will see you like that."'

She combed her hair and wet her hand again while I waited to drip dry. Patting her hair in front of the mirror with her wet hand, she said, 'And one day someone did see her. It was the joiner who had come to mend the window sash. The bathroom was at the far end of the corridor and he had nowhere else to go except towards her. She'd started to pee so she couldn't do anything except stare at him.'

We laughed and I pulled my knickers up.

'Aren't you going to wash?' Mum asked.

'No, I'll just be filthy.'

'All right.'

I leaned against the door and waited while she powdered her nose. 'I'm sorry to keep you,' she said. 'Do you mind if I just put on some lipstick?'

'No, no.'

'I got this in Queeniestreet. It's not bad but I've only got to lick my lips and it comes off. It's a bit harsh in this light,' she said, looking at herself. 'Come on then. Ready?'

'Ready,' I said, and unlocked the door.

12

AFTER THE BOOK SHOP and the Newmarket we had samosas and tea and warm, syrupy jalebees in a café off Chouringee. It was an Indian cafe, not westernised like Flury's, and the people sitting at the other formica-topped tables looked briefly at us with interest but it wasn't the invasive staring we got in Vishnapur.

'Shall we go home now?' Mum asked, as she finished her tea.

'I suppose so. I like Calcutta.'

'So do I. Sometimes I wonder if we'd been here instead of Vishnapur, whether things wouldn't have worked out better.'

'If the poverty's too much for you in Vishnapur, what would you feel here?' We'd passed a dead beggar in Howrah station, half-propped up against a pillar.

She looked thoughtful. 'There would be more things for me to do here. A big city's different from a town. I wish you could find a job here. You could work – I know – you could work at that Catholic clinic round the corner and come here for lunch every day. I could come in on the train and meet you. Have you ever thought about nursing?'

'I'd faint at the operations,' I said.

We took a tram and clanked and rumbled slowly back to Howrah. It was early afternoon but there were still crowds at the railway station and we searched the departures board for our train. There was nothing on it to tell us what we wanted

84

to know. We went on to the platforms and hunted for the right train. Other were doing the same and when a muffled voice spoke over the loudspeaker everyone stopped to listen. Neither of us understood what was said but there was a sudden surge to another platform and we went with it.

A train was standing, full already.

'Vishnapur?' Mum asked through the windows.

'Vishnapur,' came the reply. 'Yes, Vishnapur.'

Mum took us to a Ladies compartment which was slightly less full than the others. We stood near the door, jammed amongst women of all sorts and ages. As the train slowly moved out, a young man jumped on and pushed his way in. Another followed and stood holding on to the pole at the open doorway.

'Ladies compartment,' several women said crossly.

The men stayed where they were.

'Ladies,' the insistent ones repeated.

'Ladies compartment,' Mum said to the one near us at the door, and gave him a push. The train was still moving slowly. But he held on, ignoring the shouts around him.

Mum pushed again and then tried to unhook his fingers from the pole. 'Ladies only!' she shouted.

He hung on, looking out of the door. As the train speeded up, he pushed his way into the compartment. Mum grabbed his arm but he shook her off. Other women began complaining and shouting.

Suddenly there were shrill screams as the men began to fight. The open area around the doorways miraculously cleared a space. Women scrambled and climbed on to the seats to get as far away as possible. Mum and I were separated. She got pushed into the crowd but I had to struggle to keep away from the men. One of them squatted on the floor, his arms over his head. The second man beat him on the head with a shoe. After the first frenzy of beating, he paused. The squatting man brought his arms down slowly and looked about him in a dazed way, his face blank and timid. Blood came out of his eye and trickled down his face. When it reached his mouth he wiped it away.

Then the second man brought out a short thin knife from

inside the belt of his trousers, we screamed louder. He was calm and deliberate, unaffected by the noise around him. The squatting man didn't look up. He continued blinking, wiping blood from his mouth. The man grabbed his hair and yanked his head back and stabbed him in the chest. He gave a thin shriek of astonishment, and was stabbed again.

I thought I heard Mum's voice somewhere behind me, but it was distant and muted. It faded away. All the noise faded and became indistinct. Suddenly I felt my arm gripped in a blood-stopping clutch. The woman next to me buried her head on my breast and moaned. I laid my head on hers and breathed in deeply. The smell of coconut oil was so strong it made me feel sick. But it brought me out of my faint.

The train slowed down as it approached a station. The man on the floor lay on his back in a spreading pool of blood, his legs bent under him. I didn't know if he was dead or not. His arms were twitching convulsively. The other man stood in the doorway, unconcerned by our clamour. When the train had slowed sufficiently, he jumped off and ran down the embankment. When it stopped, we poured out; there was a trail of blood on the platform from our feet. People on the station came to see what was going on. I pushed my way towards Mum. She was helping an old peasant woman off the train, hauling her large sack-wrapped bundle onto the platform. The woman had a boy with her who was carrying a wicker basket full of frantically clucking chickens.

'Political, political,' people murmured, as they stared into the carriage.

Mum took my arm and we walked down the platform. Some women were crying, others jabbering hysterically, recreating the fight to eager listeners. Others, like us, were standing in a daze. An older man came up to us.

'You are from Vishnapur College?' he asked in English.

We nodded.

'I am going also to Vishnapur. Next train coming soon.' He was dressed in a dhoti and a white kurta, crumpled after the day's work in the office. 'Political,' he said, and shook his head. 'Most shocking. We will depart before the police arrive.' He had thin grey hair and a sagging, jowly face, full of concern for me.

'She saw it?'

'She was right at the front. I couldn't reach her.'

'Poor girl.'

He ushered us on to the next train. There was a rush for it as nobody wanted to be around when the police came. He stood next to us, squashed up against everyone, but careful not to touch us. When we got to Vishnapur he walked out with us to where the rickshaws stood.

'Poor girl,' he said again.

Mum stroked my arm gently. 'Thank you very much,' she said to him.

He shook his head sideways, still upset, and turned and went his way.

The next morning we searched the newspaper for a report of the murder. We finally found it in a small paragraph on the foot of page four, 'Incident on commuter train.' It concluded that the motive had been political.

'Is that it?' I said.

'That's it,' Dad replied. 'Not much, is it?'

13

I RUSHED OVER AFTER breakfast to tell Anjali about yesterday's incident, forgetting, in my excitement, the cold way we had parted. But she listened in rapt attention and then sent Lucky out to play. For half an hour she told me stories about local rapes and murders. They sounded lurid and unreal and I felt uncomfortable at Anjali's relish of all the details.

'I'm taking Lucky to the Shiva Maila this afternoon. Do you want to come?' Anjali asked when she had run dry. 'It's in the bazaar not far from here, next to the Shiva temple.'

'All right. I'd like that,' I said. 'We used to go to that before. Has it changed?'

'It's better now. You wait and see.'

We set out at four o'clock and as we walked through the bazaar children called, 'Memsahib, ta-ta!' to me. I tried to ignore them but Lucky put her little hand to her mouth and giggled. Anjali grinned too.

The Shiva Maila was a fair in honour of the god Shiva where women pray to his disembodied lingum for fertility. I knew that what they worshipped was what it represented, but it must make the men feel great to have everyone bowing down and praying to what they've got dangling between their legs. I wonder how they'd feel if it was a cunt instead. They've got the yoni, which is a cunt, but it doesn't look like one, usually just a smoothly rounded stone. You don't see it much in the little temples or at the foot of trees where people pause for prayer. A proper cunt would be a stone with a slit in it, and a little white dot for the clitoris. But you couldn't worship a thing as private as that. It's best left where it is, dark and secret. It hadn't brought me a whole lot of pleasure. Nothing but trouble, really. I didn't know what to do with the damn thing, open it up to all comers or keep it clamped shut.

The maila took place in a clearing next to the white temple. There was a huge tamarind tree in the centre of the clearing and around the outside were life-sized papier mâché tableaux of incidents in the god's life.

'Aren't they wonderful?' Anjali said.

I was surprised at her enthusiasm. As a Catholic, she had always been slightly scornful of the Hindu customs but now here she was, full of admiration. I followed her around as she carefully explained what each one meant. Lucky seemed equally awed.

'That's Shiva's wife, Parvati, riding the bird, Garuna. Kali is an incarnation of Parvati, the goddess of destruction. I wish she was here too. You'd like her. She stands on the demon's body and in all her arms she is holding the heads of those she had defeated. She has a black body and her red tongue sticks out and around her neck she wears a string of skulls.'

'I remember Kali,' I said.

'You've just missed the Kali festival. That's too bad.' She spoke as if I had no idea of what went on. But I remembered these things vividly and I liked Kali too.

'And here's Shiva sitting in the mountains with the river Ganga coming out of his head. Shiva is the source of the holy river, which is the source of life itself.'

'I know.'

'That's why the Hooghly is holy – because it's a tributary of the Ganga.'

'I know that. I've always known that.' Who did she think she was talking to?

'And there's the lingum, the source of all his creative power,' she said.

'Yes, I remember,' I said irritably.

People milled about, admiring the statues. They stood in little

89

groups before each tableau and described to each other what was happening. A thin old woman in a faded green sari was going from scene to scene, bowing and praying.

'Where's Lucky?' I said. 'I can't see her.'

'Oh, she'll be somewhere, it's all right. Leave her.'

'But I can't see her anywhere.'

'She'll be looking at the stalls. I told her I'd buy her something. Just leave her. It's nice not to have her hanging around for a while.'

But I searched anxiously about me for the little girl. Finally I saw her amongst a group of people around a stall selling bangles.

'There she is!' I cried in relief.

'I told you there was nothing to worry about.' Anjali returned to her statues and stood in silent rapture. I couldn't understand what was going on.

And then suddenly I did. Anukal was a Hindu and Anjali was soaking up anything to do with him, all for his sake. I felt irritated with her. Her face was limp with a vapid admiration. When we reached the final scene, she wanted to start all over again.

'You can if you want to,' I said, 'but I'm going to buy something for Lucky. Look, she's by the sweet stall now.'

Anjali looked vaguely in that direction.

'I get so sick of her. I'll be glad when she starts school. She's been moaning at me all day.'

'You stay here and I'll go and buy her some sweets and a toy. How about that?'

She sighed heavily. 'No, I'll come with you. I feel bad about the way I've been shouting at her today. I'll buy her something to make up for it.'

We went over to the little girl who pulled her mother towards a pile of sticky sweets, black with flies.

'Not those ones,' Anjali said, shortly. 'Ones that have wrappers. How many times do I have to tell you?'

The child whined and insisted and I saw Anjali's face tighten with anger.

'Look at these ones, Lucky,' I said quickly. 'These lovely red ones. How many would you like? I want to buy you something nice. What would you like your Auntie Hannah to buy you?'

'Those ones.' She pointed adamantly at the sticky pile but I bought the wrapped sweets and handed the bag to her. She threw them onto the ground. Anjali snatched at her arm and hit her several times. As the girl roared and cried, Anjali picked up the bag and walked away. I followed, pulling Lucky with me who went limp and had to be dragged along the ground. I wanted to smack the girl myself.

'I'm going to buy some bangles,' I announced firmly and dragged Lucky over with me to the stall. The old woman selling the neatly piled glass bangles grinned at the crying girl. Then we settled down to the serious business of choosing bangles for me.

The woman took my hand and pressed and squeezed and manipulated it, getting it wet with sweat as she pushed the bangles onto my wrist. A few broke in the attempt and these were thrown to the ground. I chose four each of several colours. I felt the weight of them on me and listened to the jingle they made and saw how the light from the stall lamp reflected in the colours of the glass.

'Now you,' I said to Anjali. 'Let me buy you some.'

Anjali chose red and green and the old woman approved. These were the colours of a married woman.

'How about blue as well?' I asked. 'And yellow?'

'No, Lucky can have those ones.'

'Will you, Lucky? Would you like some bangles?'

The girl had calmed down. Anjali took a handkerchief from the sleeve of her sari blouse and blew Lucky's nose and wiped her eyes in a hard and unsympathetic way. Lucky accepted it all stoically and then put her arms out to be fitted for bangles. She got tiny plastic ones which delighted her but she wasn't satisfied yet.

'You said you'd get me a toy,' she said to her mother.

Anjali hesitated.

'You said you would.'

'I don't feel like it any more. You've been a bad girl.'

'I'll get her one,' I said. 'Would you like a doll?'

Yes, she wanted a doll. A man indifferently sold us a red clay doll about eight inches high which Lucky clasped in her thin, dark fingers but five minutes later she dropped it and it broke into several pieces.

Anjali went into a rage. 'What am I going to do with you?' she screamed as Lucky sobbed over her broken doll. 'We're going home now and it serves you right.' She yanked her along, jerking her arm with its new bangles and shaking her thin little body. I followed them.

'This is what they do. They ruin your life. Don't get married. Don't have children. Whatever you do, don't have any children,' Anjali shouted to me over her shoulder.

We came to a main road and across from us was a fancy goods store. I said to Lucky,

'Lucky, would you like some sunglasses?'

She stopped crying. 'Oh, yes,' she said, sniffing. 'Where can we get those?'

'Let's ask in that shop over there,' I said. She ran across the road and a cyclist nearly knocked her down, shouting angrily at her as he wobbled on his bike.

'You see?' Anjali said to me. 'You see what it's like?'

We followed her and watched as she rushed into the shop and ran over to the man behind the counter.

'Have you any sunglasses for me?' she asked him earnestly.

He smiled down at her little face. 'I might,' he said. She followed him as he went over to a corner and pulled out a box with half a dozen in them.

He handed her a pair and she put them on and then turned to us. They had orange plastic frames and she tilted her head back to keep them on her little nose. 'Auntie, can I have these ones?'

'Yes, you can.'

Anjali looked down at her. 'You like them?'

'Yes, Ma.'

'You look very grown-up.' She pushed my purse away and took out money from hers. 'I want to pay.'

Lucky walked ahead of us, keeping her head back stiffly, and

92

every now and then she pushed with her finger against the bridge of her nose. She wore them seriously, refusing a sweet I offered her.

'If I'd known she'd be like this, I'd have bought her a pair at birth,' Anjali said.

She came to the flat the next afternoon, while Mum and Dad were having their sleep.

'Are you coming out?' she asked. It was what we said as children.

'Where shall we go?' I asked.

'Let's go to the water works again.'

I wasn't enthusiastic but Vishnapur didn't offer much choice. People usually came to the College.

As we walked silently, I caught her looking at me a few times. I had to keep slowing down. Indian women walk as if they've got all the time in the world. It was irritating to have to keep to her slow pace while she ruminated on something.

We took up our positions in the temple and she started her drawing in the sand, her chin resting on her knee. A crow hopped into the temple and regarded us with a bright eye. I like crows but she threw a stone at it and it hopped outside.

'Have you ever been in love?' she asked abruptly. 'All your boyfriends, did you love them?' She drew a long line.

I'd wondered this myself. Here I was, twenty-nine, pregnant, and still waiting for the grand passion of my life. I had a feeling I wasn't the type for passion. The passionate people I knew always made fools of themselves but didn't seem to mind. I did too, but I minded a lot.

I cleared my throat self-consciously. 'I don't know. At the time, I must have felt something for them, but I don't think it was love. The thing is with me, when someone wants me, then I'm not interested any more.'

'Why not?'

'I like the chase, you know, trying to get a man to like me. But it made me miserable all the time. It's so stupid.'

'But love,' she said. 'You must have loved someone.' She drew another slow line.

'There was one man.'

'And?'

'That wasn't happy either. He had a medical problem.'

She looked at me. 'What kind of medical problem?'

I didn't know the Bengali for sex. I only knew fuck which Bheme's son, Shankar, had taught me in the bushes behind the playing fields and I couldn't use that on Anjali. 'He couldn't do it,' I said. 'You know –' I was coming across as coy, which I didn't want to be.

She grinned at the floor and then looked at me sideways, expectantly.

'We couldn't even touch. He said he could only express himself in that one way and because he got terrible pain even when he got excited, we couldn't talk about it. I didn't understand it. It wasn't only – you know. I phoned him up one day. I felt I'd burst with unhappiness if I didn't say something. So I phoned him up and said I loved him. He said to wait till he was well before talking about that. I felt a bit stupid. He made me feel dumb and stupid. I don't know if I loved him or not.'

'I come here with Anukal,' she said and looked towards an area that was smooth and swept clean. 'But don't tell anybody. Please. You mustn't tell anyone – not even your mother.'

Who was she kidding, poor soul, in a place where the concept of privacy barely existed. Everyone was squashed up together in one or two rooms; each house was crammed up against the other and there weren't even any bathrooms where you could shut a door. A young woman was bathing under a tap in the street once as we went by in a rickshaw. She was rubbing soap over her sari, keeping her eyes shut and making out that there was nobody around but her.

Everyone must have known, even Anukal's jungly village bride.

'I won't tell anyone,' I said.

94

'I love him,' she said. 'I've loved him for years. He's my real husband.'

Sex after marriage with another man was one thing in this country – so long as you were discreet. But before marriage - well, that was quite another. You were spoilt then. That's what they said, like shoddy goods, used once and no good for anyone else.

I shifted slightly and brushed away some sand from under me. The afternoon sun was bright outside but the river looked cool in its brownness. The crow came back. Outside on the river bank three mynah birds pecked about. Three for a girl, I thought. A fourth fluttered down and joined them. Four for a boy.

'I've never loved anyone like that, like you and Anukal. I wish I had.'

'What happened then? How did you get pregnant?'

I stared at my feet. A breeze stirred the dry leaves of a small tree overhanging the river. The crow's feet scratched on the stone floor as it walked about.

'How did you know?' I managed to ask.

'When you wrote to your mother and said you had been in hospital. We guessed. Did you give the baby away?'

She was looking at the floor. She picked up a stone and flicked it at the crow.

'We? Who is "we"?'

'My mother and me. We talked about it. We just guessed from the way you wrote, like it was nothing at all. But we guessed it was something.'

'Did you talk about it with my mother?'

'No, of course not.'

She was being very casual, flicking stones like that. It died at twelve weeks. That's why I was in hospital.'

She finally looked at me. 'It died?'

I didn't have a word for miscarriage. I held my hand a few inches away from my stomach.

'Oh, when you were carrying it.' She looked away again and flicked another stone outside. 'So you were pregnant.'

Shani must go about her work and look at Mum and think

to herself, you've got a spoilt daughter. Mine ain't wonderful but at least she's married.

'When you lost the baby, had you tried to get rid of it? You know, with knitting needles or anything like that?'

'Oh, no. That baby I wanted. I thought that if I had a baby then it would give me something to do, to be, you know, a mother. But after I lost it, I realised that was stupid. Just because you've got a baby that doesn't mean that all of a sudden you're going to change into a wonderful person who suddenly has a role in life.'

I wanted to ask her about knitting needles.

'So he finally managed it?' she asked.

'No. No, he didn't.'

'So there was someone else?'

'Yes.'

'Who?' she asked, cupping a stone.

'Just a man.'

'Of course it was a man.'

'He wasn't important.'

'Has he got you pregnant again?'

'No. That's someone else.'

'Aree. All these men.' She spoke with incredulity. I felt pretty dirty myself.

'Yes, lots of men,' I said.

She got up and brushed down her skirt.

'I've got to get back. Lucky will be awake now.'

I followed her out.

'Are all women like you in the West?' she asked after a while.

'Pretty much.'

'So it's true what they say,' she said.

'Yes, it's true.'

'I didn't used to believe it. I thought of you and I didn't believe them.'

'Well, now you know.'

We walked the rest of the way in silence and at my gate I said, 'I'll see you, then.'

'Yes, I'll see you.'

I realised, watching her walk away, that I had come here expecting her to be on my side, to say, that's OK, these things happen. But she was an Indian with all their prejudices. She came from another world. I had forgotten that.

14

To my surprise, she came back that evening. Dad answered the door and brought her into the sitting-room. 'Are you coming out?' she asked.

'What a good idea,' Mum said. 'You go for a walk. It's a lovely night. How is Lucky?'

'She's fine, Memsahib.'

'That's good. She's a strong little girl.'

'Yes. Thin but strong,' Anjali said.

'Does she wear you out? They do at that age.'

'She does a bit.'

'And she's studying, I hear,' Dad said, standing beside her with his hands in his pockets. She smiled up at him. She'd always liked him, even if she was a bit scared of him. There was a lot to like. When he asked a question like that, he really wanted to know.

'I want her to do well in school. I want her to be a teacher like Hannah.'

'Yes,' Dad said. 'And she's clever, is she?'

'I think she'll do all right.'

'But what are you going to do?' Mum asked, leaning forward.

Anjali looked at the floor and Dad jingled some change in his pocket.

'Memsahib,' Anjali said, still looking at the floor.

'Could you not just go back to him? Would that not be easiest in the end?'

'No,' she said. 'No, I want a divorce.'

There was a silence.

'And then what?' Mum asked gently. 'How will you manage without a husband?'

I felt embarrassed for Anjali, having to answer Mum's questions with all of us watching her.

'I could work,' she said. She swallowed and said quietly, 'Maybe Sahib . . .' He bent towards her, his hands still in his pockets, to catch what she was saying. 'Maybe, Sahib, you could find work for me in the office. I have my school certificate.'

He jingled his change again. 'I'm afraid people ask me that all the time. Men with families . . .'

'If Memsahib could write a letter,' she said, raising her head and looking at Mum, 'I could be an ayah in Calcutta.'

Tears came into Mum's eyes. 'I don't know. You've got your own child to look after.'

'I can send her money. I can save up for her.'

'If that's all you can do, then I'll write you a letter. But surely he's not so awful.'

Anjali looked at the floor again. 'I feel sick every time he touches me,' she said.

Dad cleared his throat.

'We'll go now,' I said, and took her arm.

We went out of the gate and I led the way in the other direction, past the main compound. There was the smell of Queen of the Night in the air, sweet and seductive, and cicadas clicked away busily. We went on to a grassy patch by the river where other couples were sitting, men and women close but not touching, hugging their knees. Bats flitted in the warm, moist air.

She tore blades of grass to pieces. I waited for her to speak. 'The thing is, you see . . .' she said in a whisper.

'What?' I said, stiff and apprehensive.

'What we were saying before. You know, at the temple.'

'What about it?'

'There's something you don't know.'

'There's a lot I don't know,' I said.

'About me.'

'So tell me.'

'I'm surprised you haven't guessed already. Guess what it is.' She chewed a blade of grass.

'I don't know.'

'Think. Think back to what we were saying.' She tugged at the grass, pulling up handfuls. I didn't like guessing games. I ducked as a bat swooped near my head and then I remembered the knitting needles.

'Are you pregnant?'

'Yes.'

'Oh, I see. I see. Yes, I see now.'

I felt tears welling. I still had a friend. The relief was overwhelming. I wiped my eyes but the tears kept coming. 'I thought you found me dirty,' I whispered.

Hearing the tears in my voice, she looked round and then pulled my head down on to her shoulder. I cried while she smoothed my head.

'Dry your eyes. Use my sari,' she said. She dabbed my face gently with the end of the thin cotton sari which smelled of the sun. 'I was shocked, it's true. I never thought of you like that. But you've come along like an answer to my prayers.'

I laughed weakly.

'No, it's true,' she said. 'I have to get rid of it.'

'How far along are you?'

'About three months, I think. It may be more. I can't wait much longer. It's starting to show on my thin body. I've heard about a clinic in Calcutta but I'm too afraid to go on my own. I don't know what kind of questions they'll ask. But if you were with me, I wouldn't feel so afraid.'

I wiped my nose with the back of my hand.

'Will you come?' she asked anxiously.

I pulled up handfuls of grass.

'What is it?' she asked.

'I should get done too.'

'How far along are you?'

'Only eleven weeks. No, it must be twelve now. Or is it more? I can't remember.'

100

'It's getting on.'

There were wee boats on the river, fishermen fishing at night. You could only make them out by the little points of light in the middle of their boats.

'When you lost that baby you told me about, did you see it?' she asked.

'Yes. I held it in my hand.'

'How big was it?'

'This big,' I said, outlining the length of my palm.

'And what did it look like? Did it look like a baby? Do you think it felt anything?'

'It was dead,' I said. 'It couldn't feel anything.' It had had a white backbone and a wee curled arm but I couldn't bring myself to tell her this.

'I imagine mine coming out of me. Is it still alive when it comes out? Or does it die when it's being pulled out? Or after it's out, like a fish.'

'Don't think like that. It's best not to think about it. Does Anukal know?'

'No. You mustn't tell him.'

'You should tell him.'

She picked a piece of grass. 'What can he do about it? Have you told anyone?'

'Oh God no.'

She sighed and then looked at me sharply. 'Is that why you cut your hair?' she asked.

'No,' I said. 'No, that's got nothing to do with it.'

'Oh,' she said and chewed on the grass.

'Do you have to make an appointment?' I asked.

'I don't think so. I think you turn up and if they can do it that day, then fine. If not, then you come back the next day. You have to get there early.'

'Can you wait a few days? I'll come with you on Friday.'

'Why? What will happen in that time?'

'It'll give me time to think.'

'About what?'

People walked by on the road behind us from time to time,

101

their sandals scraping on the rough tarmac. Even those in bare feet padded by, not silent. A group of people paused in their talking and I felt them looking at me. They carried on talking but their voices were lowered with a tone of intrigue.

'I'd like a baby,' I whispered. 'I'm getting old.'

'But if you have a baby, you'll never get a husband. A man doesn't want a spoilt woman.'

'I don't know if I want a husband.'

'Really?'

Those bats were lovely, flitting dark against dark. A soldier bugled the last post from the cantonment across the river. I imagined a flag coming down slowly and men in heavy boots clumping back to barracks.

A husband tied things up neatly and conveniently. You fitted in, you were a woman with a man, just as it should be. You could sigh with relief and say, I've done it. Look, Mum, I've done it after all.

'But don't you think there are men around who won't mind if I have a baby already?'

She snorted. 'Maybe in your country but not in this one. And what would your parents say? How would they feel? You'd shame them.'

'I know.'

'How would you work? Where would the money come from?'

'Isn't it lovely though, to have a baby?'

She took the end of her plait and pulled at the hairs. 'No, it isn't. It's not what they say. If I didn't have Lucky things would be much easier for me.' She chewed on the end of her plait. 'Don't have a baby,' she said. 'A baby will ruin your life.'

'There's not much to ruin,' I said.

'What will your school say when you come in to class every day, getting bigger and bigger?'

'I'm not going to teach any more.'

'Ay yai yai,' she said and spat out some hairs. 'And I thought my life was difficult.'

'It is,' I said. 'You've got more problems than me. Look.'

102

I held up my hand and counted off on my fingers. 'You're pregnant. But married to someone else. Your marriage has failed and you're stuck with your parents. If they find out about you and Anukal – never mind the baby – what'll they do?'

'They'll throw me out.'

'Right. So there's you out on the streets and your daughter at home crying for her mother –.'

'She won't cry for me.'

'And I guess you won't cry for her.'

'No,' she said. 'No.'

'That's another one then,' I said. 'A whole hand's worth of problems.'

'OK,' she said and held up her hand. 'You're pregnant. You've got no husband. You don't love anyone –.'

'A man,' I said. 'I don't love a man. There's lots of other people I love. Well, a few anyway.'

'You don't have a man to love. You want a husband.'

'That's the same finger,' I said. 'You can't put that one on two fingers.'

'There's plenty more to go,' she said, putting back one finger. 'You've got a good job but you want to give it up. You've got no money.'

'But I won't end up on the streets,' I said.

'So where will you end up?' she asked, pausing over the thumb of her second hand.

'God knows.'

'Right,' she said and ticked it off. 'And you walk around with no hair.'

'Anukal liked my hair.'

'He likes anything you do,' she said.

'Does he? What does he know about me?'

'Not a lot,' she said and laughed.

15

I HAD FIVE NIGHTS OF lying awake and thinking, until the whole question didn't seem real any more. I woke up in the mornings too tired to go to chapel and lay in bed and listened to hymns that I had sung as a child. I looked at Mum but that made it even more unreal. I knew what she'd say. She'd say, have the baby and I'll come back with you and help you look after it.

She'd say, Hannah, Hannah, oh Hannah. What have you done?

Mum came back with me when I was eighteen and we lived together for a year while I got settled in to a new country. I didn't like the new country. We were on a bus one day and Mum looked out of the window at a car below us and said,
   'I dream of you marrying a man with hands like those.'
   It was a bright green car and resting lightly on the steering wheel was a pair of hands with long, elegant manly fingers. I tried to see his face but it was hidden by the top of the car. The lights changed and he drove on.

We sat in the dark corridor with fifteen other women. It was above a bicycle repair shop and we listened to the tink tink tink of metal on metal as something was banged into place. I had to ask for the toilet. It was the usual filthy hole and I had to step carefully, others had been here before me, even though it was so early.

When I got back to my seat the woman opposite me said to Anjali, 'What's she doing here?'

'Same as you,' Anjali said.

She smiled at me. She had a plump face and small, friendly eyes. I managed a smile back.

'Tell her not to be frightened,' she said. 'This is my fourth time and there's nothing to be frightened of.'

And there was me thinking I looked cool and calm.

A door opened and a woman in a white sari came out and distributed forms for us to fill in. She looked at me suspiciously.

'What do you want?' she asked.

That floored me. I'd have said an abortion, only Anjali hadn't given me the Bengali for it. There was a woman in the other room sitting behind a desk.

'You are a journalist?' she asked me in English.

'No, I'm a patient,' I said shyly.

She looked me over.

'Come here,' she said. She was efficient looking in a brusque way with black horn-rimmed glasses.

I went over to the desk, clutching my form. She leaned sideways to look behind me and said to the women, 'If you can't read and write come over here and the nurse will fill in your forms for you.'

Some women came over and stood around me.

'We are a charity, you see,' she said to me in English. 'We only ask that those who can pay, do so.' She looked at me rather coolly.

'I'll pay,' I said eagerly. 'For me and my friend.'

I pointed to Anjali and she looked over at her.

'She is your friend?'

'Yes, she is my friend.'

'How is this?' she asked.

'We grew up together,' I said. I felt about ten years old.

'She is your servant's daughter?' she asked.

'That's right,' I said.

She smiled to herself as she looked down at the papers in front of her. Then she looked up. 'It's nice you have a friend,' she said.

When it was our turn, Anjali and I were led into a big bright room with two netted windows that faced onto the street. Scooters, taxis, cars, buses roared and spluttered, people walked by talking and laughing, music blared cheerfully from the radio downstairs. Curtains divided the beds. The nurses wore white saris and I saw a doctor with an ordinary sari and a white coat over it. A sweeper walked through the room with her sari hitched up over her ankles, carrying an aluminium bucket full of dirty water.   I was shown to a curtained cubicle. As I stood wondering what to do, a nurse came in.

'Put it on, put it on,' she said, pointing to a thin, worn white gown on the bed. She left and I undressed and put it on, feeling more than naked.

The doctor suddenly appeared, pulling the curtain back and making me jump.

'Lie down,' she said. She had a big mole on the corner of her mouth. The indifferent nurse stood at my head, watching the doctor. My pubic area was washed with something smelling antiseptic and then the doctor pushed a cold instrument up my vagina. I stiffened and the nurse put her skinny arms on my chest and pushed me down.

'Relax,' the sharp-faced woman between my legs said in English. 'Loosen your muscles. It will help a lot if you do. Breathe now, breathe for me. In, out, in, out. Slowly, that's it. Slowly.' As she talked the instrument pushed harder and more painfully. It was sharp and cutting, ripping at my insides.

'Come on, now,' the sharp-faced woman said. 'There's not so much pain. Relax, relax. Your friend has more pain. She is much further on than you. Yes, that gave you something to think about, eh?' She called over her shoulder to someone and another nurse came in with a tray of instruments. I put my head back and shut my eyes and the nurse at my head leaned more heavily on me.

'It's all over now,' the doctor said and the nurse let go of me. 'Everything has come out, placenta and everything. It's good. It's fine.'

I turned to the side and vomited. The nurse tutted in irritation and called to the sweeper who came in with her bucket. Then I was handed a glass of water and I drank it greedily.

'Slowly, slowly,' the doctor said and I vomited again. The nurse handed me another glass and angrily forced me to sip.

Then the two of them got me to stand. There was a movement between my legs and I looked down and saw a bloody cloth on the floor. The nurse tutted again and pointed to it. I picked it up and held it between my legs. They took my arms and guided me into another room where mattresses were laid out around the walls.

After a while, some hours, the doctor came into the room. She stood at one end and said, 'Lie on your backs. I'm going to examine you.' A nurse stood beside her with a large aluminium bowl in her arms. The doctor put on a pair of rubber gloves with a snap and then dipped her hand into the bowl. She knelt down beside the first woman and her hand disappeared under the white gown. The woman drew in her breath.

'Fine,' the doctor said. 'You can go.'

She dipped her hand into the bowl and moved on to the next one. When she reached Anjali I turned my head away and found the woman next to me regarding me with interest.

We got dressed and they gave us thick sanitary towels to stuff in our knickers and then Anjali and I were on the street. The men in the bicycle shop looked at us with sly, knowing eyes.

Anjali hobbled beside me.

'Stand up straight,' I said.

She made a little effort and I did too, and then she hobbled again, as if she were carrying something between her legs. We got a taxi to Howrah and made it back to Vishnapur by early evening. We took a rickshaw from the station and when it stopped at the main gate she got off without a word.

'I'll see you,' I said.

'Yes,' she said, not looking at me. I knew she was thinking of home and the one room and everybody there.

Mum and Dad were reading the paper, just having had their dinner.

'Did you have a nice time?' Mum asked.

'Yes,' I said and sat down as my legs began trembling. 'Well, actually, I got a really heavy period.'

Dad rustled his newspaper.

'Oh dear,' Mum said sympathetically. 'Do you want to lie down?'

'Yes, I think I will. I feel rather sick.' I got up and went to the bedroom and Mum followed me.

I lay down on my back and she turned the fan on. I watched the blades turn very slowly and then gradually get faster as the lovely cool air reached me. She sat on the edge of the bed and looked down at me.

'When did it start?' she asked.

'A few hours ago.'

'Did you find a toilet to go to?'

'Yes.'

'Was there any water? Could you wash yourself?'

'Yes, there was water.'

'That was lucky. Do you want to wash now?'

'No, no.'

I turned my head away and she stopped her questions. I turned back to look at her and her face was thoughtful and regretful as she looked over my head at the window. She became aware of me watching her.

'I'm sorry it spoilt your day with Anjali.'

'Yes.'

'You'll have other days.'

'I know.'

She sat on. The room was dark and the fan whirred round on the ceiling. I shivered.

'Do you want the light on? Shall I get you an aspirin?'

'No, I don't want anything. I feel sick.' I wanted her to go.

She got up and put the light on.

'I don't want the light on,' I said irritably and she turned it off.

'Do you want me to go?' she asked.

'No, no, that's all right.'

Dad cleared his throat in his study and Roshan clattered dishes in the kitchen. Mum sat down on the bed and it creaked slightly under her weight. Hugh began barking in the lane and she got up and went to the window.

'Go away, Hugh!' she said.

He barked up at her.

'Go away! Go on, shoo. Be quiet. Shoo! Shoo!'

'It's OK, Mum. Never mind.'

She came back to the bed.

'What a silly name for a dog,' I said. 'Especially a Bengali one.'

Hugh barked again and a dog from the bazaar barked back.

'Do you remember another night like this many years ago when I had a terrible period?' I said.

'In the boarding house that night just before we sailed?'

'I was so sick,' I said and thinking about it I felt even sicker. 'I kept going backwards and forwards to the bathroom and I remember passing Dad's bed and wondering how he could sleep through it all. I bet he wasn't asleep.'

'I bet he wasn't. It was the monsoon and Bombay was flooded,' she said.

'And we waded through filthy water in the streets. I thought it was great fun.'

'I was worried that you were ill from that water.'

'I remember there were three or four women in saris who

were squatting by the side of the road, peeing. I was really shocked by that.'

'I don't remember.'

'But when they stood up and walked away I saw by their faces that they were men. I was quite relieved. It's funny,' I said.

'What is?'

'That I was more shocked at the thought of them being women and having a pee than at them being men dressed up as women. They must have been those dancers, you know, the ones that sing and dance at weddings, the eunuchs. Shows how Indian I was. It's OK for men to be eunuchs but not for women to pee by the side of the road.'

'Yes,' Mum said vaguely.

Ganga called out to Lalu down below and he answered her a little irritably from Jamuna's side of the compound.

'What does Deedi mean?' I asked.

'Deedi? It means older sister. Why?'

'Lalu and Bheme call me that. Why older sister?'

'It's a sign of respect. I didn't know they called you that,' she said.

'It's strange, though, for men to call me that.'

'They can't call you Missahib because you used to play with their children. Well, I suppose they could. But Didi is nice. It means you're part of the family.'

I turned my head but she bent closer.

'Are you tired?' she asked.

'Yes.'

'Why are you crying? What is it? What's the matter?' She bent so close I could feel her warm breath on my cheek. Then she clapped my head and tried awkwardly to hold me.

'I don't know.'

She got up to bring me a hankie.

'You're tired and not very well,' she said. 'Shall I leave you to sleep for a while?'

'Yes.'

'I'll look in later. Just shout if you want anything. I'm not far away.'

'I know.'

'You'll have another day with Anjali.'

She finally went, shutting the door quietly behind her.

16

'ARE YOU BETTER NOW?' Mum asked me at breakfast. 'It's still very heavy. There's blood on the sheet so I've put it in to soak in a bucket.'

Dad's eyes wandered over to the window.

'You're very pale,' Mum said. 'Do you want to stay in today? I'm judging an elocution competition. I wondered if you wanted to come.'

'Elocution?'

'It's the students. Mrs Kershaw began it. They seem to like it.'

'Why?' I asked.

'Why what?' Dad said.

'Well, it just seems odd.'

'Why odd?' He leaned over the table towards me and I made an effort not to lean back.

'I don't know. I suppose it isn't. It's a bit unexpected, that's all. Yes, I'll come.' I didn't want to be alone today.

It was held in the main hall of the library and the large, dark, book-smelling room was filled with theology students. Mum and I and Mrs Kershaw sat at the back.

'Will you introduce it, Isabel?' Mrs Kershaw asked. She sat with her hands in her fat lap and her feet, crossed at the ankles, barely touched the floor.

'I thought you were going to do that.'

'Go on,' Mrs Kershaw said with a little laugh, settling further into her chair and clasping her hands together.

Mum stood up and walked to the podium at the front. An expectant silence fell over the students.

How beautifully she talks, I thought, as she explained in a low, quiet voice to the students what was going to happen and told them to speak slowly and clearly and not to be nervous. Her cheeks were slightly flushed and there was a lovely diffidence to her as if disclaiming any right she had to be there telling them what to do. At the same time her ordinary words were lit with sincerity. Oh, how I loved her. I looked down at my lap to hide my tears.

When Mum returned to her seat, Rahul stood up and went to the podium. I found myself smiling, pleased that he was here.

'They asked me,' he began, looking over at Mum and Mrs Kershaw. 'They asked me to start off.' He was holding a book and his eyes went from the book, to the floor, to the students and back to the book. 'A demonstration.' He hesitated and opened the book at a marked place and then closed it again. '*War and Peace*,' he said, smiling. For all his hesitation, there was confidence in his manner.

He began to read. It was the part where Natasha and Andrei meet up again after the battle of Borodino and Andre is dying and she asks for his forgiveness. He read quietly with great feeling and simplicity. When he read, '"I love you," said Prince Andrei' the students roared with laughter. He waited for the laughter to die down and carried on as before. He came to 'I love thee more, better than before' and they laughed again, slapping their thighs and rocking in their chairs.

I tried to block out the laughter and concentrate on Rahul's almost feminine mouth. I leaned forward, wanting to smash the heads of all these stupid men who collapsed in hilarity at the word love. A thought crossed my mind and I looked for Khup Lalzrom but he wasn't here. No, he wouldn't be.

Rahul read on, his eyes lowered, his small hand slowly turning the page and smoothing it down as his eyes went to the top of the page; he continued without faltering. Yes, I'd go and see him. I felt tears rising again. I shouldn't have come.

'I'm going back,' I whispered to Mum when Rahul had finished. I left as one of the students began a ponderous reading from the Bible, closing the door behind me on the hushed, respectful silence.

Outside, the place was busy with students. I stood on the top step and looked down the tree lined entrance way to Anjali's house. I didn't really want to see her but felt I ought to. And I wanted to see how she was managing.

'Are you there?' I called, not from the inner door but from the verandah. No barging in on family scenes again.

Lucky came running to the door and smiled expectantly at me.

'Hello, Lucky. Where's your mother?'

'I'm here,' Anjali said, and stood at the door with her back a little bent.

'How are you?' I asked.

'Terrible.'

There were black circles under her eyes and she walked ponderously over to the verandah door. I thought she was overdoing the suffering bit.

'Did you sleep?' she whispered.

'A little.'

'I didn't.'

'What did you say to your mother?' I asked.

'About what?'

'About why you were bleeding so much.'

'I didn't say I was bleeding.' She looked at me incredulously. 'You said . . . ?'

'Yes', I said. 'I had to say something.'

'I said nothing.'

Lucky stared up at us, her little woman's eyes suspicious. She tugged at her mother's sari and Anjali pushed her away roughly. She tugged again and Anjali slapped her and she ran into the house, sobbing.

'She won't leave me alone,' Anjali said.

'Let me have her for a few hours.'

'You? What would you do with her?'

114

'I don't know. Play with her. I'll find something. I'll enjoy it. Let me have her.'

She looked at me doubtfully for a moment. 'All right,' she said and then went into the house.

'Come on,' she said to the girl. 'You're going with Auntie Hannah for a little while.' She sat her up, wiped her eyes and her nose with the end of her sari and smoothed down her dress. 'Now you behave. Will you be a good girl?' The girl nodded. 'Will you do everything she tells you?' A nod again and a shy look at me. 'If you don't, I'll beat you. Auntie Hannah will tell me if you're naughty and you'll be punished. Won't you?' she said, turning to me. Lucky watched me too, with an anxious little face.

'She won't be naughty, I'm sure.'

'She had better not be.'

We walked over to the flat, her bony little hand in mine.

'Auntie,' Lucky said.

'What is it?'

'Where do you live?'

'Just here. See up there? Just there.'

She looked up, trustingly.

Dad was on the back verandah, drinking coffee.

'Hello,' he said in surprise. 'That was quick.'

'I wasn't feeling all that well.'

'Oh.' He looked at Lucky. 'You've brought a friend.'

'Who's this, Lucky?' I asked.

'It's the Sahib,' Lucky answered promptly.

He sat in his chair and smiled at her, almost mischievously. 'Would you like a biscuit?' he said. He picked one up from the plate and handed it to her. When she reached out for it, he pulled his hand away. Lucky laughed and grabbed for it, but she was too slow. He held it out for her again and she half reached for it, not wanting to finish the game by getting the biscuit too soon. Her wee ugly face sparkled with excitement. It was like two old children playing a game. He gave her the biscuit and Lucky held it, looking hopefully at him for more.

115

'Again,' she said. And he did it again. When she got the second biscuit she wanted the fun to go on.

'No,' he said with a smile. 'I think that's enough.' His arms resting on his chair, he waited for me to take her away.

'Eh, what's this?' Shani said. She came through the verandah door from my bedroom with a brush in her hand and quickly ushered us away. We went back into my bedroom and sat on my bed.

'What are you doing here?' Shani asked Lucky. 'Have you come to play? Eh, have you come to play?'

Lucky smiled at her and Shani smiled back, a long, slow smile of love.

'Are you going to show me how you can write?' I asked her. I got up and found some paper and a pencil. But when I gave the pencil to the her, she refused to use it properly, scribbling instead all over the paper.

'Will you draw me a picture?'

No, she wouldn't. She scribbled again and then looked around her. She explored the wardrobe and opened drawers and looked in the bathroom. The bathroom fascinated her and she turned taps on and asked Shani to show her how the shower worked. She wanted to use the toilet so I lifted her onto the seat and she solemnly peed into it.

'I think God has sent you,' Shani said to me as we watched the girl.

I was too astonished to reply. I lifted Lucky off the potty and we returned to the bedroom.

'Her husband has written,' Shani said. I jingled my bangles. Lucky climbed onto the bed and began counting them. 'Go and look in the wardrobe,' she said to Lucky. 'Show me what you can find there.' The girl jumped down. 'He says that if she doesn't come soon, he'll divorce her.' She whispered the word divorce so low that I nearly missed it.

'Does she know?' I asked.

'Not yet. What if she says she wants a divorce?'

Lucky's skinny legs stuck out of the wardrobe as she sang a tuneless song to herself.

'She won't listen to me,' I said. 'What can I say to her?'

'If he divorces her, it's the end.' She jerked her chin towards the little girl. 'She'll have nothing, no father, nothing.'

'I need to do pee pee,' Lucky said, emerging from the wardrobe.

'But you've just been,' I said.

'I need to go,' she said, dancing about in desperation.

I lifted her on to the potty again. She produced a few drops.

'She's got plans for Lucky,' I said, lifting the girl off.

Shani shrugged. 'Plans. When do plans work out? It's this Anukal business. Don't think I don't know about it. She's told you, hasn't she?'

We sat back on the bed. I looked down at my lap. 'A bit.'

She shifted closer. 'What does she say?'

I jingled my bangles again. 'Nothing much.'

'Not how she feels about him? What she thinks she's doing? Anything like that?'

Lucky was trying to shut herself into the wardrobe. I opened the door and pulled down a blouse for her to try on. 'Nothing like that.'

'She's never grown up. I thought that having Lucky would bring her to her senses.' She looked fondly at the girl who was putting on the blouse. 'You want everything for your children.'

'Come here, Lucky, I'll do up the buttons,' I said.

She watched Lucky admiring herself in the mirror. 'What happened yesterday?' she asked, looking at the girl.

'Yesterday?'

'When you were in Calcutta.'

'Nothing much. We had a nice day. Let's find another blouse, Lucky, a smaller one.'

Shani stood up. 'I'd better get on with my work. You be a good girl now,' she said to Lucky. 'I'll take her home with me when I've finished.'

'OK.'

She came for her an hour later. We had been playing with

117

my make up and the wee girl's face was gaudy with colour. She looked like a misshapen clown. Shani dragged her into the bathroom and washed her face. Lucky cried and struggled and then she cried all the more as she was pulled towards the front door.

Dad came out of his study to see what was going on.

'Goodbye,' he said to her.

'Look, you've disturbed the Sahib,' Shani said with an embarrassed face.

'You'll come again, Lucky,' I said, but the girl's screams could be heard all the way down the stairs.

Mum returned when Roshan had just finished setting the table for lunch and we sat down and waited for it to be served.

'Who won the competition, Mum?'

'Khup Lalzrom.'

'But he wasn't there.'

'He came late.'

'He always wins things. Couldn't you have given the prize to someone else?'

'If someone's good, they win,' Dad said. 'He happens to be very clever.'

Roshan brought out the plate of rice and the bowl of cauliflower curry and set them down before Dad.

'But not good,' I said.

'What do you mean?' Dad asked, his spoon poised above the rice.

'I mean about that business with the girl.'

'That's another matter altogether.' He served out the rice and the curry and handed me my plate. 'It's nothing to do with this competition. Do you want him to lose because of that?'

'Yes,' I said, defiantly, knowing it was a stupid thing to say.

To my surprise, Dad had no answer. He spooned out Mum's lunch.

'I know what you mean,' Mum said, pushing her fork around

in the rice. 'But there wasn't anyone else half as good as him. Except Rahul, of course. He was asking after you.'

'What did he say?' I asked, concentrating on my lunch.

'He wanted to know why you left. I said you weren't feeling very well.'

'I enjoyed his reading.'

'You'll have to tell him that.'

'I might,' I said, avoiding her eyes. 'I liked the piece he read.'

'It was my idea,' Mum said. 'I've always loved that bit from *War and Peace*.' Her eyes got red and watery. 'Where they come together again and he forgives her and says he loves her now more than ever.'

I loved it too but I kept my face stiff as I ate my lunch.

'So he hasn't read the book?' I asked.

'No, I don't think so.'

That was disappointing. But it only took away a little from my vision of him.

17

As I wasn't well, Mum brought Paul Tulp over to entertain me. She asked him for tea on a day when Dad had a meeting.

'I hear you have been judging babies,' he said, in a pleasant foreign accent.

'The ugliest baby won,' I said, but it didn't sound funny any more.

The man laughed. 'Things always happen the wrong way round in this country.' He said it as if he liked this aspect of Indian life, unlike the German who would have been sarcastic and dry. He sat holding his plate, his legs crossed and his eyes flitting between me and Mum. He addressed his remarks to her.

'Have a piece of cake,' Mum said, cutting a slice.

'Yes, please,' he said at once, and held out his plate. He was thin and reserved, not at all like a cake-eater.

'Paul has been to England,' Mum said.

'Is that where you learnt your English?'

'No, I knew that before. I went to visit only. I worked as a waiter in a restaurant to get some money and then went hitch hiking around the country.'

'Where did you go?' Mum asked.

'To many places. To Cornwall, to Wales, to the Lake district. I liked this place the best. But Wales was nice too. I tried to leave it on a Sunday but it was closed.'

'What was closed?' Mum asked.

'Wales,' he said, and we laughed at his joke politely. He pushed his thick blond hair back from his face.

'It's true,' he said. 'I had to stay an extra night. There were no trains, buses, nothing. I had to sleep in a ditch but oof it was uncomfortable and cold. I tried to sleep by counting muttons and even that did not work.'

He was puzzled by our laughter. We explained and he smiled agreeably, shrugging his shoulders.

When the visit was over we saw him to the door. He crossed the hall to his door and rang the bell.

'I hope he is in,' he said. 'I don't have my keys.'

We waited to see. The door was opened by a young Indian man with a thin moustache and eyes that glanced furtively sideways.

'Ah, you are in. Good. I don't have my keys,' Paul said to him in English.

'Who was that?' I asked as soon as we had shut the door behind us. He didn't have the appearance of a servant.

'That was Jeremiah,' Mum said with a little smile.

'Get away.'

'I know. But it's true. His name is Jeremiah.'

'What does he do, this Jeremiah?'

'He's his servant. But he seems to be a friend as well. Paul found him when he was studying in Poona.'

'Found him?'

'We don't know much about him. Dad calls him his manservant. How are you feeling now?'

We were standing in the dark corridor.

'Not too bad.'

'I'm glad you're still friends with Anjali.'

'Yes.'

'Shani talks a lot about her. We both talk about our daughters. We've stuck together through thick and thin, Shani and I. She's my friend.'

'Yes, I know.'

'It's good to have a friend.'

'Yes, it is.'

Footsteps echoed up the stairwell. They passed our door and carried on.

That evening, I stood up from my chair in the sitting room. 'I thought I'd go next door and borrow some books from Paul on Hinduism,' I said.

Mum and Dad looked up from their newspapers.

'All right, dear,' Mum said.

My heart beating uncomfortably, I rang his bell; regretting it at once, I wished I could run away.

He looked surprised to see me. 'Come in,' he said, smiling politely at my ear. He led me into his sitting-room and turned on the lights.

It was bare and grey-looking with nothing on the walls. There were three light bulbs in the huge room, yellow and naked. He had a wooden sofa, like ours, and two wooden arm chairs centred around a little table which looked awkward in its attempt at homeliness. There was nothing on the table and no cushions on the chairs. At the unlit end was the same large table as ours with two chairs.

We stood under one of the light bulbs. 'Please,' he said, pointing to a chair.

'I would like to borrow some books of yours on Hinduism,' I said, not sitting. I felt painfully transparent.

'Of course, of course,' he said, looking relieved. 'They're all in my study. I'll find some for you.' His face, sharp-nosed and aloof, cheered up a little.

I followed him into his study. He was wearing a shirt that could have done with a wash and a green lungi that was tightly wrapped around his slim hips. The light was already on in the study. Books lined the walls.

'Ah, but have you read them all?' I said, laughing.

'Oh.' He shrugged and smiled, unsure of the joke.

There were books and papers on his desk, neatly laid out, no scholarly passion here. An orange packet of Charminar lay beside a full ash tray. 'I'm sorry to disturb you,' I said.

He glanced at his desk and then began to search his

bookshelves. 'Here, this one is a good introduction.' He handed me a paperback. 'And this one too. It's not bad. It gives a good grounding in the history – if you can say it has a history. Nobody knows how or where it began, you know. It is so ancient.' He gave me a third and then a fourth book.

'This should do me for now,' I said.

He continued his search. 'There is one book that I know you will enjoy, if only I could find it. Let me see. It gives a good intellectual treatment of Hinduism. Ah, here it is.' He handed me an enormous hardbacked book. 'It is not all about idols at the foot of trees, you know.'

'That's all I know about it,' I said. 'And praying in the river and blowing conches that wake me up at four in the morning.'

'There is a reason for those conches,' he said seriously.

'And for four in the morning?'

'And also for four in the morning.' He smiled. 'Read and you will find out.' He was doing his best to be jovial, poor soul.

'I suppose so.'

'Yes, indeed. You read those books and you will know almost as much as I do.' He raised his shoulders and gave a little giggle.

'I don't know if I want to know all that amount.'

His shoulders dropped. He looked at his feet which were bare and rather grimy from the cement floor. They were pleasant feet, strong and shapely. Did he wash them every night before he went to bed? I wondered what his sheets were like.

He edged towards the study door.

'There are so many aspects to Hinduism,' I said. 'I never realised that when I was growing up.'

'Children just see what is before them,' he said, looking at the front door. His hair fell over one eye. He pushed it back.

There was a pause while I watched him look longingly at the door.

'Well . . .' he said.

'Do you like it here?' I asked.

'Here?' He looked at me. 'Where here?' He spoke like an Indian. 'In Vishnapur?'

'In India.'

He looked me full in the face and I thought I was getting somewhere. Then he dropped his eyes.

'Of course.'

'But why?'

He shrugged. 'Why do you like a place? You just do. You like something, you don't like it, it just happens. There are no answers.'

'I think there are answers,' I said.

'Why do I like it. Let me see.' He looked at the pile of books in my arms and his long nose caught the light and shaded his thin-lipped mouth. 'Because there's nowhere else,' he said, young and almost boyish with his sudden, painful honesty.

'Nowhere else?'

'No, there's nowhere else.'

'There's nowhere else for me either,' I said.

A key sounded in the door and he turned to it with a relief he didn't bother to hide. Jeremiah came in and Paul said,

'Ah, there you are.'

'Hello,' I said to the young man. He smiled in an abashed way, mumbled something and sloped past us down the corridor and into one of the bedrooms.

'Thank you for the books,' I said.

'I hope you enjoy them,' he said and opened the door for me.

'Good night,' I said.

'Good night,' he replied, through the half shut door.

This is me now, empty and childless, I thought, in the stillness and familiarity of the church service on Sunday. Mr Kershaw, fumbling and apologetic, swayed in the pulpit of the shabby Portuguese church. I waited for regret. I tried to bring up an emotion but none came, only an undercurrent of trembling.

I went to see Rahul that afternoon, after lunch. I felt furtive and shy on a visit on my own to a man in a country where you just don't do that, not where you can be seen anyway. The large, quiet grassy courtyard of the student hostel was empty and I had to ask Shadu Lal, the gardener, where Rahul's room was. Everyone else was asleep.

'Up there, on the first floor,' he said, pointing to a door behind the verandah. His normally cheerful face regarded me solemnly and I felt his eyes on my back as I climbed the stairs.

There was a long pause after I knocked on the door and I was about to turn away when a voice said, 'Come in,' in Bengali.

I opened the door and went in to an empty room. There was a movement from a doorway to my left and Rahul said, 'Oh, it's you,' standing in his trousers and vest, looking tousled and sleepy.

'I'm sorry. I'll come another time.'

'No, no. Sit, sit. I'll just . . .' and he disappeared into his bedroom for a few minutes and came back with a shirt on and his hair brushed and smelling of cloves. It was a lovely warm, rich smell and I wondered for the first time what it would be like to kiss him. But the thought disappeared as soon as I looked at his lips and I felt embarrassed to have caught him in this little act of vanity.

'You're not sitting. Sit here, look,' he said and drew up a chair for me at the small table where I could see that he sat to eat his meals and write his lectures. He sat opposite me and so the table was between us. Outside was bright and dazzling and inside was cool and grey from the cement floors and the dull white walls. Clothes hung on hooks on the doors and there were books stacked up lazily on the floor.

'It's very quiet,' I said.

'We all sleep very quietly here.'

'I forgot about sleeping. I'm sorry.'

'Stop apologising.' He stood up and I stiffened slightly. 'I'll make you tea,' he said. 'You want tea?'

'Yes, I want tea.'

As we drank our tea sitting across from one another, his eyes darted around his rooms. He sat back in his chair very at ease even though I was sitting stiffly and sipping self consciously.

'My father is coming for a visit soon,' he said. 'I shall have to tidy up.'

'I remember your father,' I said.

'What do you remember?'

'A thin, ascetic man with a gentle smile.'

'Gentle smile. That's how you see him? I suppose,' he said. 'When he comes he stays for two days just. That's how long we can stand each other. Not like you and your parents.' He looked up from the table and I smiled but he didn't.

'It was engineering that I was going to do.' He watched his hand as it smoothed the table. 'Arshdeep went into the air force and Naresh is doing something with computers and that left me. He never said he wanted one of us to do theology but I knew. So I did it.'

'Does it make him happy that you've done this?'

'I think so.'

'And you?'

'You have to understand,' he said. 'When he converted to Christianity he had been married two, three years so he was a young man only. He was a Brahmin and you know what Brahmins are like.'

'Yes, I know.'

'Everything must be done inside their caste and if so much as the shadow of a sweeper touches them then they must have a ritual bath.'

'To cleanse them. Yes, I know. I know that.'

He glanced at me. He was holding his heavy white china cup in both hands, leaning back in his chair.

'When he converted he wanted to do something to show his conversion, to make it mean something. So he went out one morning and touched a sweeper.'

'How did he feel?'

'He felt disgusted, of course. But every day he touched one

126

until he got used to it. Just touch. Like this.' And he leaned across the table and laid his hand on mine.

It caught me unprepared but it was the briefest of touches, slightly damp.

'And that's why you did theology?'

'I don't know. I suppose so. Why did you do teaching? Does it make you happy?'

'I couldn't think of anything else to do and no, it didn't make me happy.'

'Didn't?'

'I've given it up.'

'So now you have nothing. Not even something to make you unhappy.'

I looked at the table and wanted him to touch me again.

'I'm looking for something.'

'Good luck,' he said, still not smiling.

'I'd better go back now,' I said and waited for him to say, come again. But he didn't. I left him at the door and when I turned around at the top of the stairs to give a wave, he wasn't there.

18

THE FLAT WAS SILENT when I got back. Mum and Dad were still asleep. I leaned on the front verandah railing, smoked a cigarette, and thought how nothing was able to touch me any more, not even Rahul with his firm little hand. The more I thought about his touch, the firmer it became. All that was left in me was dust and sand like the road below where people walked, unconcerned. I turned at a slight movement in the almond tree. A vulture sat on a thick branch.

It shook its heavy black wings to balance itself. Shocked, I stared at its weighty beak and its bald, curved neck. A child called from the road below, 'Eh, Memsahib!' and, distracted, I turned to see who it was. But it was just a child, a grinning little boy in baggy shorts. When I turned back to the vulture it had gone.

Surely I would have heard its wings beating and the bough would have shaken as it pushed itself off. I stood there for a long time, wondering and afraid.

There was a ring at the door. I didn't want to answer it, to speak to anyone. There was a long pause and it rang a second time. Dad came out of the bedroom and went to the door. He led in Mr Ramamurthy, the bursar, from downstairs. I came into the sitting-room and Dad gave me a filthy look. He didn't like his afternoon sleep interrupted.

Mr Ramamurthy looked agitated. He stood under the fan,

took off his black horn rimmed glasses, and wiped his face with a handkerchief.

'You will not believe what has happened to me,' he said. 'It is hard for me to believe it myself. I will sit, if you don't mind.'

He dropped his heavy body onto the wooden sofa and I waited expectantly.

'I think you should go,' Dad said to me coldly. 'Mr. Ramamurthy may wish to speak in confidence.'

'No, no. Not in confidence,' he said. 'Not in confidence. But you will find it shocking. It is this Naga girl, the ugly one with the squinty eyes, Nudy Hemrom. We had a disagreement in the class. I always mark fairly and her work did not come up to standard. She is not so clever, Mr Walker, this you know. She said I had marked her too low . . .'

'Was this in class?' Dad asked.

'Yes, exactly, in the class, in front of everybody, standing there so bold. I said to her, I have not marked too low, I always mark fairly. And she said to me, "I want to suck your blood."' He looked at Dad. 'Just like that. "I want to suck your blood." I had to sit down. I told her I would report her. She went banging and crashing out of the classroom.'

I looked at Dad and could tell from his eyes that he was loving this.

'Banging and crashing?' he asked.

'Making a most terrible noise.'

'Would you like me to speak to her?'

'I don't want her in my class any more. She will have to be transferred into another class. Maybe into Rahul Prakash's. I refuse to teach her now.'

'Well, we'll have to discuss this. I'll speak to her. If she were to apologise – ?'

'I don't want to speak to her again. What is there to say? I have told you everything. Those are the facts and there is nothing more to be said.'

'There are always two sides to an argument. In fairness I'll have to hear her side.'

Mr Ramamurthy breathed heavily and stared at the carpet.

He took his glasses off again and wiped his face with his handkerchief.

'You must do what you think best,' he said, finally.

'I'm sorry you're so upset,' I said.

'Thank you,' he replied. He stood up and said to Dad, 'I will wait to hear from you,' and left.

'That wasn't what he wanted to hear,' I said. 'He wanted you to be shocked and say how awful these Naga students are.'

'I suppose it is pretty awful,' he said, smiling. 'I wouldn't like to suck Ramamurthy's blood.'

'Nor would I.'

We heard Mum get up and Dad smiled to himself. When she came into the sitting-room he crept mysteriously towards her and hissed in her face, 'I want to suck your blood!'

'What?' she said, stepping back warily, while Dad and I laughed.

'I want to suck your blood!' he hissed again, and we told her the story.

'What are you going to do?' Mum asked.

'Ask her not to do it again. And if she apologises then maybe he'll let her back in the class.'

'But he said he wouldn't,' I said.

'I think he can be persuaded.'

Roshan and Shani let themselves into the flat and shook their sandals off at the door. Roshan raised his eyebrows at the three of us standing in the sitting-room.

'Do you ever get vultures in that tree out there?' I asked.

'Oh, vultures and blood! That's enough,' Mum said, looking upset.

'But do you?' I had to know.

'I don't know what's wrong with you these days,' Mum cried. 'I just don't know.'

'What's wrong with me? What about you?'

She walked out of the sitting-room. 'Don't bother about me,' she said angrily. 'Look to yourself.'

'What about you?' I shouted after her as she ran into her

bedroom. I followed her as far as the corridor. The door slammed and I shouted again, 'What about you?'

I stood trembling outside the door and Dad walked past me and went into the bedroom and shut the door behind him. I didn't want to hear their muffled conversation so I went to my bedroom and, standing by the window, waited for the tears to come. But they didn't. Cry, damn you. Cry. Mum can do it at the drop of a hat. Why can't you?

Shani crept into the room. 'What's going on?' she whispered.

'Mum's upset about something.'

'I know that. But what?'

'I don't know. Dad's in with her now.'

'No, he's just gone back to his study.'

'Is she still in the bedroom?'

'Yes.'

I looked out of the window.

'I think I'll go in to her,' Shani said.

'All right.'

The two women came out twenty minutes later, Mum red-eyed and carrying her bag. I followed her as she went towards the front door.

'Where are you going?' I asked.

'To Calcutta.' Her lips were tight and she wouldn't look at me.

'Calcutta?' I asked feebly.

'Yes,' she replied angrily and slammed the door behind her.

I felt angry too. I went to find Shani who was hanging out clothes on the back verandah.

'What's going on?' I asked.

Shani smiled in a self-conscious and embarrassed way. 'Give her time,' she said.

I was aware that Dad could hear us from his study. Shani probably was too.

'Time for what?' I asked reluctantly.

'To sort herself out.'

She pegged up a pair of Dad's grey and shapeless underpants.

131

'Well, I don't understand it. I'm going to see Anjali,' I said.

Anjali was sweeping the yard in front of her house, resting her free hand on her bent back as she swept with long even strokes. She straightened up as I approached.

'I saw your mother go off in a rickshaw,' she said.

'I know. She's gone to Calcutta.'

'Why?'

'I don't know.'

'She looked upset.'

'She was.'

'My mother watches me from the corner of her eyes.'

'They know something has happened and they're angry because we haven't told them.'

'How do they know?' Anjali asked.

'They just know.'

'Come, and we'll talk.'

'Over by the bushes?' I said.

'Yes.'

We went to the corner of the playing-fields up against the high jute mill wall and pushed our way through the bushes and sat down in a small clearing.

'Lucky comes here sometimes. She found it by herself,' Anjali said.

'Already?'

'I know.'

'Do you remember?'

She looked down at the earth and smiled. 'I remember,' she said.

We came here when we were about ten or eleven and lifted up our skirts to one another to examine each other's budding and bursting genitals. I had wanted to go further and touch but Anjali wouldn't let me. All that shameful curiosity which no amount of looking could satisfy.

'I know what you and Amit did in our kitchen,' Anjali said, tearing a leaf off a bush.

Dear God. I felt shocked and my face went hot and red and

132

almost throbbed with embarrassment. All those years ago, a thing that I had kept hidden and secret, pushed away into a dark cave and anxiously examined every once in a while. My dreadful secret had never been a secret after all.

'When we played hide and seek,' Anjali said. 'You and he always hid in the kitchen.'

'Is this you just guessing?'

'No. He told me.'

'When?'

'At the time.'

I could feel his penis, damp with sweat, rubbing squeakily against my bum. That was all that happened. Me with my back to him and him doing what he wanted to do and I let him, not knowing what it was that he wanted.

'Why did you do it?' Anjali asked, looking at me sympathetically, one woman to another, women who had put childish things behind them.

'I don't know,' I said. 'Because he wanted to. I wasn't afraid of him or anything. I didn't want to. I didn't even know what he was doing. He never hurt me or, you know, did anything to me.'

'So what did he do then?'

'Just rubbed up against me from behind.' Was I going to blush again? No, I wasn't. My face felt cool. 'There was one time, not in the kitchen. He was flying a kite in the playing-field and it was some time after he had said that he didn't want me to play with him any more because boys don't play with girls.'

'Except in the kitchen.'

'There was no one around and he said, well, he said what he always said to me.'

'What?'

'Do you want to do what we do in the kitchen?'

I laughed but she didn't.

'I said no, but he kept asking, so I said yes, and he tied the end of the kite string to the tennis post and we came here.'

'Was this before or after us?'

'It was only because he didn't want to play with me that I began playing with you.'

'And here we are now,' Anjali said.

'Yes, here we are now.'

'Go on.'

'Well, we sat down and he took it out, you know, and he kept saying, touch it, touch it, but I wouldn't. It looked such a horrible thing. And then this little cloud of white stuff came out, like a mushroom, I thought, and he looked embarrassed. Then he let me fly his kite for a while.'

Anjali chewed a leaf and then spat it out.

'How old were you when your mother told you about men?' I asked her.

'She never told me.'

'Mum and I were in Calcutta when I was about nine or ten and we passed a prostitute. She had lovely lipstick on and I asked Mum why she was standing there. I saw her hesitate as if she was deciding something, and then she told me.'

'What did she say?'

'About how the men come and kissing and all that.'

'And paying for it?'

'I don't remember that. Just how they did it.'

'But don't you remember that Jamuna and Padma and everybody had told you?'

'Yes, but I never believed them.'

Anjali laughed.

'I only asked Mum about the woman because I liked her lipstick.'

She laughed again. 'So that's why you never wear lipstick. Look at your mother with all her reds and pinks.'

She tore another leaf apart and chewed at the stem. 'I told Anukal about the abortion.'

'What did he say?'

'He said I'd done the right thing.'

'Bastard.'

Anjali contemplated me for a moment. 'Bastard,' she said. 'Bastard, bastard, bastard.' Then she covered her mouth.

134

The bushes rustled and Lucky appeared.

'There you are,' she said and sat down next to me. I put my arm around her and she cuddled up to me.

'Auntie,' she said.

'What is it?'

'What are you doing here?'

'Just talking.'

'About me?'

'No, not about you. About when your mother and I were little girls, like you.'

Her thin old little face looked up at me. 'You were never like me.'

'Oh, but I was,' I said.

'Was she, Ma?'

'I suppose so,' Anjali said, chewing on another leaf.

19

D AD AND I HAD tea on the back verandah, and I was very conscious of being in Mum's place in this ceremony. I poured out tea and handed him milk.

'Thank you,' he said gravely.

We heard Mum come through the door and waited for her to appear on the verandah.

'Would you like some tea?' Dad asked.

'Yes, please,' she said, sitting down, quiet and a little chastened.

I still felt angry towards her so I didn't ask her where she had been. She was back too soon to have gone to Calcutta. She drank her tea in silence.

There was a ring at the door and Roshan went to answer it. We heard his growl and his feet slapped back to the kitchen and then a doubtful voice called,

'Mr Walker?'

'In here,' Mum cried. She had recognised one of the Naga students and rose to welcome him.

Two men came on to the verandah, smiling and bowing and laughing in their shy, agreeable way. They were Thangzalien and Dalien, third-year students.

'We have come about the cat,' Thangzalien said. He was an older man from Burma, and every year he crossed the Indian border illegally to come to the college. He had a serene, sensuous, experienced face.

'Oh, the cat,' Dad said.

'The cat?' I asked.

'It is not here?' Thangzalien asked, smiling gently.

'Well, no, actually we haven't caught it yet,' Dad said.

'Yes. We saw it as we came in. It is at the front.'

'I suppose now would be as good a time as any,' Dad said, half rising from his chair and looking at Mum.

'Yes, now,' she said, and Dalien laughed. He was younger, with a big mouth and crooked teeth and thick, spiky hair.

'We will catch it,' he said and they left with Dad.

'What cat?' I asked Mum.

'Chappati. It belongs to Keislar but he doesn't want it any more and so the Nagas want to eat it.'

'They've come to eat the cat?'

'Don't tell Roshan. He thinks badly enough of the Nagas as it is.'

'Poor Chappati.'

'I know. But what could we say? They're very hard up. We couldn't say no and then just leave it to wander about.'

'I suppose not,' I said.

'They have cat and dog markets.'

'It's a tough old cat. There can't be much meat on it.'

Dad returned with the students and the cat, a big brute of an animal, grey and stripy. He carried it slung over an arm and stroked it with his free hand.

'It came very quietly,' he said, putting it down on the floor.

The cat looked around suspiciously and then walked over to the far corner and the students followed it. Mum and I retreated to the corridor and Dad followed us.

'What shall I do?' he whispered. 'Shall I stay? Do you think I should stay?'

'I don't know,' Mum said, her hands on her cheeks. 'I don't care.'

'Maybe I should stay,' he whispered.

We heard a growl from the verandah and Dad said, 'Yes, I think I should. Do you think – ?'

But Mum and I fled to the front door, leaving Dad with his

quandary. We stood outside the door and waited, looking at the floor.

'What a long time they're taking,' I said. Mum remained silent and I wished she'd say something. I tried not to think of the cat and what they were doing to it. Ganga came up the stairs and stopped in front of us.

'Are you all right, Memsahib?' she asked.

'Yes, I'm fine, fine,' Mum said.

I smiled and Ganga smiled back, puzzled. She carried on up the stairs to Morag's flat, looking back doubtfully.

Finally the students came out of the door, carrying a package wrapped in newspapers.

'Thank you,' they said, smiling and bowing, not obsequious but polite and graceful.

We found Dad in the sitting-room, looking pale and with a gin in his hand.

'It took ages,' he said. 'He had such a thick strong neck they had trouble breaking it. But I think I did the right thing by staying. They seemed to appreciate it.'

We sat down with Dad. 'I have to prepare a lecture on ethics but I don't really feel like it at the moment,' he said.

It was nice to see Dad like this, with his little weaknesses.

'I have a problem,' Mum said.

'Would you like a gin?' Dad asked.

'No,' she said, and looked out of the window in that annoying way she had of grabbing your attention and then making you wait.

'What is it, Mum?'

'I want to go home, David. I don't want to stay here any longer. I'm not doing any good here and I'm wasting everyone's time and it all seems so useless. I think I'll go back with Hannah.'

'I don't have a home to go to,' I said.

'I just can't stay here any longer,' Mum said, as if she hadn't heard me. She spoke in a low, quiet voice with her head bowed over her hands which rested in her lap. The way she spoke and her resolution to be honest seemed false and put on.

'This isn't something you can make your mind up about in a hurry,' Dad said.

In a hurry? Where had he been these last few weeks?

'Maybe you could go back with Hannah and have a holiday and a rest and then come back again. You could help Hannah find a job.'

She raised her head and looked at me. 'Yes, I could do that. I've been so worried about you.'

'Don't worry about me, Mum. Worry about yourself.'

'I've been very selfish. Thinking about all my problems and here you are with no job.'

'I'll be fine, Mum. What about you? Why are you so unhappy?'

'I don't know. I really don't know.' She began to cry quietly.

'I don't think running away will help anything. I think you should stay, Mum. Really, I do. Stay and see this one out.'

From the way Dad was looking at her, I knew that this had come up before.

'You used to love it here, Mum. If you go away . . .'

'If she goes away, what?' Dad asked.

'Well, it'll always be there.'

'What will?'

'Whatever it is that's troubling her.'

'We don't know what is troubling her.'

'I want to love people again,' Mum sobbed. Her fair hair fell over her face and I couldn't speak for the tears in my throat. Dad didn't say anything either. He looked at the gin in his hand.

'What do you want, Dad? Do you want her to stay?' I said. Mum's face remained covered but her sobbing quietened.

'It's not what I want, it's what she wants.'

'Let's put that to one side for the moment. What do you want?'

'What's best for her.'

'Oh Dad.'

'Of course I'd rather she stayed,' he said, almost angrily. 'But that's not the issue here.'

139

'Maybe you should both go back,' I said. There was a silence.

'I don't think that would solve anything,' Dad said.

Mum sniffed and wiped her eyes. We waited for her to speak. 'I'm sorry,' she said. She got up and left the room and we heard her go into the bathroom and wash her face. Dad got up slowly and hesitantly from his chair, glanced at me and then went into his study.

20

S HE CAME BACK INTO the sitting-room looking red-eyed and unhappy but as if she had collected herself.

'We've got a little while till dinner,' she said. 'I'm going over to the Principal to ask if they can come to dinner on Friday. Do you want to come?'

I hesitated. 'All right,' I said and stood up. I tried to catch her eye but she bustled about, looking for her comb. 'Why are you asking them to dinner?'

She found her comb in her bag and went into her bedroom. 'We owe them a dinner,' she said, combing vigorously in front of the mirror. 'We went to them ages ago and I've been putting off asking them back. But I can't put it off any longer.'

We walked down the stairs and to the compound gate. Ganga, Jamuna and Padma were sitting on the cement bench at the top of the steps going down to the river, in the late afternoon sun. The season was getting cooler now. 'All right now, Memsahib?' Ganga asked.

'Yes, I'm fine now, thank you.'

'That's good.'

'How are you?' Mum asked.

Ganga smiled as if the question amused her. 'I'm fine. Getting too old, though.'

'You're not old, Ganga.'

'Oh, Memsahib, I feel it.'

'That's what she always says,' Padma said, putting her strong masculine hand on Ganga's shoulder.

'I know what you mean,' Mum said.

'You, Memsahib?' Jamuna's eyes skimmed over Mum and then she smiled and turned her head and neatly spat out red betel juice down the river bank.

'How's Baila doing? I wonder when she'll get pregnant.' Mum asked.

The women laughed. 'Give her time, Memsahib,' Jamuna said. 'But she seems happy enough. Everyone's happy in the beginning.'

'I wasn't,' Mum said. 'I wondered what kind of man I'd married.'

'That's so,' Ganga said. 'It takes a while to get used to a man. But you never get used to losing a child.'

Padma rested her hand on Ganga's back and Jamuna spat towards the river again.

'I've lost a few,' Padma said. A crow flapped down from the tree and began to peck at the dry almond leaves on the ground.

'I've lost a baby,' Mum said.

'Two of mine have died,' Jamuna said.

It was something that happened and the women sighed. I sighed as well and Jamuna raised an eyebrow at me.

'But you're not old, Memsahib,' Ganga said. 'You've got much life ahead of you.'

'I know,' she said unenthusiastically.

As we continued on our way, I asked, 'Were you not happy when you first married?'

'I remember once I ruffled David's hair playfully and he turned round and hit me. Not hard, just a sort of angry push. He was always tired from working but I wanted some fun. I was so upset that I ran away across the fields. But where could I go? I had to come back again.'

I had a vision of Mum leaping over fences and running through fields of yellow stubble.

I smiled. 'I can just see you,' I said.

142

'I did some pretty daft things.'

'Is this a pretty daft thing, wanting to go away?'

'Maybe. We'll see.' Her lips closed tightly and defensively and we walked in silence for a while. 'I'm going to ask Rahul and Paul for dinner at the same time. The Sens are too heavy-going on their own. Do you want me to ask Keislar as well?'

'No.'

'I didn't think so. But I thought I'd better be sure.'

There were only a few students in the compound, most of the classes being over for the day. But then I saw him. And he saw me. I didn't say anything until we were going up the steps to the Principal's flat and I stopped Mum and said,

'I just saw the man who killed that man on the train.'

'Where?'

'Just now. He must be a student here. Oh, Mum. He saw me. He saw me recognise him.'

'Sit down, sit down,' Mum said and pulled me down on to a step. We sat, huddled in the dimness.

'What'll I do?' I asked.

'Are you sure it was him?'

'Positive. Especially from the way he looked at me.'

'You didn't imagine that?'

'No.'

Our whispered voices echoed in the stairwell.

'I don't know what to do,' Mum said.

'Maybe Dad will. Maybe we shouldn't do anything.'

'We'll go back and ask him. Let's see the Sens first and get it over and done with.'

We stood up and went to the door and rang the bell. Sarasati answered it.

'You're working here?' I asked her.

'Yes,' she said, but she was stiff and formal, not wanting to talk. She led us to Mrs Sen who was coming out of the kitchen. She gave us a thin smile and then led us to a small room that looked out on to the flat roof of the portico and gestured towards some chairs, sitting down on one that creaked under her weight. Then she turned her head and called out in her rough hoarse voice, 'Tea!' Sarasati replied, 'Yes, Memsahib.'

'Oh, please don't bother,' Mum said.

Mrs Sen gave a slight sideways movement to her head but didn't cancel the tea. The welcoming ceremony over, she rested her elbows on the arms of her chair and looked at me.

'So,' she said. 'You are a teacher.'

'Yes,' I replied uncomfortably.

'Not a bad job,' she said without conviction.

'No.'

'You don't like it?'

'Well . . .'

'She likes it very much,' Mum said. 'She was always writing in her letters about the children and how much she enjoyed teaching them.'

'You are on holiday?' Mrs Sen asked, ignoring Mum.

'Yes, that's right.'

'Long holiday.'

I couldn't think what to say and waited for Mum to come to my rescue. But she was silent.

'What do your children do?' I asked.

'My son is in business in America. My daughter is with United Nations in Delhi.' She clasped her hands across her large stomach. I felt sorry for Mum with no such boast. I looked out of the open door that led onto the roof of the portico and saw the man again, standing alone near where I had last seen him. He was looking at the house.

'Who is that man?' I asked. 'Is he a student?'

Mrs Sen turned and looked. Then she looked at me with an oily smile. 'You like him?'

'No, no. I think I've seen him somewhere before, that's all. I don't know where, though. I just wondered . . .'

'He is chemistry student, final year. Mithras Choudry, I think he's called. Spends too much time in politics. A good boy, nice boy. His uncle is Congress M.P. for this area. You have seen his picture in paper perhaps.'

'The uncle?'

144

'This boy,' she said impatiently.

'Maybe. I don't know.'

As we drank our tea Mrs Sen kept giving me ghastly roguish looks. But she accepted Mum's invitation to dinner with a tight, false smile.

On our way home, I said, 'I didn't think the Congress people went in for knives and murders. I thought it was just the Marxist groups who killed one another.'

'So did I. We'll see what David says.' Mum was still very quiet. I wished I hadn't said anything about seeing the man. It only added to the turbulence inside her head. The quieter she was, the more was going on.

'I talked to one of the students yesterday,' I said. 'It was John Emannuel, I think. He was setting out for the bazaar and I asked him what he was going to buy and he said, a time-piece for alarm.'

'So he won't be late for chapel,' Mum said. 'He's taking the prayers next week.'

'The time-piece will wake him up and he'll get alarm when he remembers he has to take the prayers,' I said. She didn't even smile.

We went into Dad's study as soon as we got back and sat down on the two chairs and faced him across his desk.

'We've got something we need to discuss,' Mum said, and Dad sat back with his elbows on the chair and his hands together as in prayer. He bowed his head and touched his lips with his fingers. We told him who we had seen.

'We must go to the police,' he said, when I'd finished.

'He'll be in cahoots with the police,' Mum said. 'His uncle is an M.P. I'm more worried for Hannah's sake.'

'You think he might threaten her?'

'Yes, I do. I think she ought to go back.'

'But what about you? He'll know I've told you. And lots of people saw him, not just me. I don't think he'll threaten me.'

'I didn't like the way he was standing and looking at the house,' Mum said.

'But he'd left by the time we came out.'

'Even so. What do you think, David?'

'That's up to Hannah.'

'How can you say that? How can you sit there and say that? Her life is in danger.'

'Don't exaggerate, Mum.'

'I'm not exaggerating.'

'We should go to the police,' Dad said.

'It won't do any good,' Mum said angrily. 'You know that perfectly well.'

'I don't know any such thing. Neither do you. We have a duty to go to the police.'

'Duty!' Mum said scornfully and looked down at the floor. Then she looked up. 'We have a duty to Hannah and we should send her away.'

'I'm not a parcel, Mum. And I'm not going away. I'm not going away.'

'Why not? What's there here for you? You moon around, doing nothing. What's happened to you? Why are you like this? I know something's happened and if you won't tell me, fine. But you've got to go back, you've got to find a job, you've got to get on with your life.'

'I am getting on with my life. What do you know about it? I don't have to live out my life in front of you.'

'Fine, fine. Go and do it somewhere else.'

'We're getting away from the issue here,' Dad said.

'Oh shut up, shut up, shut up,' Mum shouted.

I let out a great wailing cry and ran from the room. I ran past Roshan who watched me from the kitchen. I ran into my room and sat on my bed, rocking back and forth, sobbing. It was true, there were no answers here. Mum followed me into the room and sat down on the bed beside me but made no attempt to touch me.

'I'm sorry,' she said. 'I'm sorry. I'm letting my own troubles spill over into yours. But part of my trouble is I'm so worried about you. Please don't cry. Please. Don't cry now. Don't cry. I'm sorry. I'm so sorry.'

But I cried on, my tears turning into a huge weeping. I cried like I'd never cried before, huge sobs taking over the whole of my body.

I was vaguely aware of Dad coming into the room.

'She's upset about the murder,' Mum said.

'Yes,' Dad said.

They murmured something to each other and I cried until I felt dizzy. Gradually I began to calm down.

'Tell me what you'd like to do,' Mum said, putting her arm around me.

'Do?' My body heaved as I drew in breath.

'About this man.'

'What are we going to do about you?' I asked in a thick, wet voice.

'Never mind me. Shall we go to the police?'

'Yes,' I said. 'Yes, we should go to the police.'

The police station was a large converted house from colonial times near the Portuguese church. It was a whitewashed building in neat grounds where the grass was clipped with precision. A clerk whose face was pitted with smallpox marks sat behind a desk in the hall and looked up at us.

'Yes?' he said in English. 'You wish something?'

'We would like to see the superintendent,' Dad said.

The clerk rang a bell on his desk that pinged sharply in the high-ceilinged room. A thin man in a grubby dhoti and a long khaki shirt appeared. The clerk said something to him and the man went away. Policemen in big khaki shorts and khaki puttees walked in and out. Dad looked around and saw a bench by the wall and went and sat on it. Mum and I sat with him. The clerk ignored us. He clenched his teeth as he wrote, his jaw muscles bulging rhythmically. The peon returned and the clerk looked at Dad.

'Please to follow this man,' he said, indicating him with his head.

'Thank you,' Dad said as he stood up.

We followed the peon down the hall and through several

partitioned rooms where men sat at desks piled high with paper. He knocked on a door and waited with his hands behind his back for a reply. A muffled voice called out and he opened it and left us.

A large, solid looking man sat behind a desk with only a few sheets of paper on it. He gestured towards some chairs.

'You are from the College?' he asked.

'Yes'.

'Your name is?'

'My name is David Walker and this is my wife and this is my daughter.'

'Sit, sit,' the man said, drawing his chair up closer to his desk to show that business had begun.

We sat nervously. I waited for Dad to begin and the man in his khaki uniform and hooded eyes waited too.

'My daughter was witness to a murder,' Dad said.

'And your daughter is?'

'This is my daughter. Hannah Walker.' It was funny to hear him say my name like that, as if I had nothing to do with him.

The man looked at me. 'When?' he asked.

'Thursday.'

'So long? Why so long?'

'There were lots of other people who saw it too. It was on the train from Calcutta to Vishnapur.'

'Oh, that one. And?'

'And yesterday I saw the man who did it. He's a student at the college.'

The superintendent sighed. 'Name of?'

'Mithras Choudry.'

He rubbed his hand wearily over his face and sighed again. He looked at his watch and then took a piece of paper out of a drawer and placed it in front of him.

'You have been at the College how long?' he asked Dad.

'Nearly twenty-five years,' Dad said, unable to keep a little pride out of his voice.

'I have seen your wife several times on a rickshaw going to the bazaar,' he said with an unexpected smile and his chin pointed towards Mum. She smiled, showing her teeth. 'You like it here?'

'We like it very much,' Mum said. 'We've spent most of our working life here.'

Dad sat with his arms and his legs crossed. He unfolded his long legs, shifted in his seat and then crossed them again.

'My daughter was born in Pakistan,' Mum said. 'She spoke Punjabi before she could speak English. Now, of course, she speaks Bengali and she speaks it much better than we do.'

The superintendent looked at me.

'You like it here?' he asked me in Bengali.

'Yes, very much. My friends are here. I feel it's my home,' I replied, also in Bengali.

He smiled. 'Good,' he said. Then he returned to English and looking down at the blank piece of paper, he said, 'You have spoken to anyone else about this business?'

'Nobody else,' Dad said.

'That is good. You must not mention it to anybody. It is a dangerous business. This much you understand?'

'We were just saying that,' Dad said. He uncrossed his legs and leaned forward to continue. But the man waved a hand.

'That much you understand,' he said. 'That is all you need to understand. Good. That is all.' I saw that we were being dismissed. I stood up and Dad looked at me and then slowly rose to his feet. Mum did too and the three of us hesitated before the man. He gave us a brief and reluctant smile.

'Namaskar Ji,' I said and his smile broadened slightly.

'Namaskar,' he said.

Then Dad put his hands together and Mum did too. Whenever Dad did this his clean white hands came flat together, lightly touching, but Mum's were more supplicating, the fingers slightly bent, the palms hollow. The superintendent grunted Namaskar to them and then put the piece of paper back into the drawer and we left.

'What a crook,' I said cheerily, once we got outside.

'Are you sure he wanted us to go?' Dad asked.

'He didn't want us there in the first place,' Mum said.

149

'He sussed us out as being pretty harmless,' I said.

'It was your Bengali that saved us,' Mum said, squeezing my arm. 'He took quite a fancy to you, and no wonder.' She was cheery too.

'So you think he knew all the time who this Choudry person was?' Dad asked.

'Yes, Dad, he knew all the time. Never mind, we've done our duty.'

We walked back along the river. The morning sun was pleasantly warm and there was deep shade under the trees where the leaves stirred and rustled slightly. A boy led three black buffalos into the river and they walked in slowly until only their noses and eyes and great heavy horns were above the brown water. The boy went in up to his knees and threw his head back and began to sing at the top of his voice.

21

AFTER LUNCH MUM LEFT to oversee Bheme as he climbed into a sewage tank to unblock it.

'Oh Mum,' I said when she told me.

'We're paying him fifty rupees,' Mum said.

Dad went to lie down for his afternoon sleep and the flat felt silent and empty. I stood on the front verandah smoking and listening to Roshan wash the dishes and put them away. Usually I liked the afternoon quiet but I felt restless and unsettled and unhappy. Roshan came and leaned on the railing beside me and I offered him a cigarette. He smoked it, looking out over the river, smoking it the Indian way between his first and middle finger and inhaling the smoke straight down into his lungs as he sucked his clenched fist.

'Eh, Johnnie Walker,' he sighed.

I laughed. 'What is it?' I asked.

He smiled, showing his white little teeth. He threw his cigarette over the railing.

'I'd better get back,' he said.

He'd never been a talker. When I was small I used to sit on a stool in a dark corner of the kitchen and chat away to him. Eh? Eh? I'd say. Isn't that so? and he'd give an occasional grunt in reply.

A moment after leaving he came back. 'There's something going on with the boy next door,' he said.

I followed him out onto the landing and we listened at the

door. There were strange sounds coming from behind the door, a voice speaking but an unfamiliar one and it sounded as though it was coming from the floor. We knelt down by the door.

'That doesn't sound like Paul,' I said.

'No, it's the other one,' Roshan said. 'His servant.' And he raised an eyebrow.

'Can you open the door?' I said in English. 'Is he a Tamil?' I asked Roshan.

'No, he's a Malayalam. Hey, open the door,' he called in Bengali and banged on it with his fist. The moaning stopped for a minute and then resumed.

I banged too and then peered through the letter box. 'I can see him. Jeremiah, open the door. Let me in. I can help you. Stand up now. That's it. Stand up and come to the door. He's coming.'

'I always thought the boy was mad. He has a mad look to his eyes.'

'Shh.'

'He's gone crazy.'

'We don't know that. Maybe he's ill.'

The door opened and Jeremiah stood with a drooping neck looking at the floor. He staggered back and I caught him before he fell again.

'Maybe he's drunk,' Roshan said and sniffed his mouth. 'No, not drunk. What's the matter with you, eh?'

'I just feel . . .' he said in English, his voice slurred as though drunk.

'What do you feel?'

His face opened out into a smile, a loose wide smile and he gazed at me with bright watery eyes. 'No,' he said. 'I have to . . .'

'What? What do you have to?'

He looked around him, his eyes slipping over Roshan and he leaned back against the wall.

'Let's get him to his bed,' I said.

We took hold of his arms and staggered with him down the hall and into a bedroom. It was stark and bare with two beds, one unmade and we lay him on that one. He gazed up at the ceiling and then turned his head slowly and smiled loosely at me again. I wished he'd stop doing that.

'There,' Roshan said. 'You sleep now. He's fine. Leave him.'

'I'll stay for a while until Paul comes back. I don't like to leave him.'

Roshan shrugged and gave the young man a contemptuous look before going. Jeremiah returned his gaze to the ceiling, the smile fixed on his face. I couldn't bear the intimacy of that loose, mad smile so I wandered around the flat. I went into Paul's bedroom, slightly less stark that Jeremiah's with a crumpled Indian bedspread on his bed and a few photographs of white people on his dressing table. Last year's calendar was on the wall, a garish view of white mountains and green trees and neat little houses. I cautiously opened a few drawers. There were shirts and underwear, nothing interesting.

Then I rummaged as quietly as I could in a messy small top drawer, listening out for Jeremiah. Near the front I found a packet of condoms. I opened the packet and tipped them out into my hand. There were five. One had been used.

Who on? On whom? Who with?

I put them quickly back in the packet and then in the drawer, hoping it was the same place I had found it.

The key sounded in the door and I rushed into the corridor as Paul opened the door.

'Hello!' he said. He looked surprised but wary and embarrassed too.

'Jeremiah isn't well,' I explained, indicating the bedroom and his shoulders sagged with relief.

'What's the matter with him?' he asked, going to the bedroom.

'I don't know. He seems to have had some sort of collapse. He's wandering and not quite himself.'

'Are you not well?' he asked the young man in jovial tones. Jeremiah lay on his back and turned his head to him and gazed with his long lashes and then he turned to me and smiled in a sickly way.

'I love you,' he said.

Paul laughed. 'What's this?'

Jeremiah's smile broadened. 'I love you,' he said again to me as if he were drunk.

'What are you saying?' Paul said, smiling and glancing at me. Jeremiah reached for my hand and I let it lie in his for politeness' sake before pulling it away. 'You'd better let her go,' Paul said. 'She's been very kind, looking after you like this.'

I left the room and Paul saw me to the door. 'Thank you, sister,' he said, smiling at me, almost coyly and not in the least embarrassed as I had expected him to be.

'Sister?'

'Of mercy.'

'Oh. That's OK. I hope he gets better.'

'He'll be fine,' he said as he shut the door.

I sat in the sitting-room, feeling shocked and also ridiculous. What a fool, what a bloody fool. I always went for the wrong bloody men. But why did I go for him? Because he was there. I didn't feel attracted towards him, I just wanted him to be attracted to me. Why couldn't I stop this nonsense, this wanting men to want me and then when they did, not knowing what to do with them. Just opening my legs, that's all I knew. Oh God, oh God.

I decided to go and find Mum. But the cement bench was empty so I sat and watched the way the river swirled with the currents. A dead cow floated past with its legs stiff and sticking out like bleached branches. It made me think of Lucky.

I went to see Anjali. Shani was there, in the kitchen in her petticoat. 'I'll see to Lucky,' she said. 'You go out with Hannah. But not for long, now. I've got too much to do.'

Lucky wanted to come and I wanted her to come as well but Anjali said, 'I've had enough of you today.'

Lucky looked at me, knowing she had an ally. I said, 'Another time, darling. I'll take you out another time.' She followed us to the gate, a little figure with legs like sticks. Shani called her back.

'We can't go far,' Anjali said. 'What is it you want?'

'Just to talk,' I said, put off by her coolness. 'Let's sit here.' We were at the cement bench.

Anjali squatted on the bench, her arms resting on her knees. She looked disgruntled and irritated. 'I had a big fight with Anukal yesterday,' she said. 'I told him what you said about him.'

'What did I say?'

'You know – bastard.' She lowered her voice. 'He was really upset.'

'Why did you tell him?'

'I don't know.'

'You said it too. Did you tell him that?'

'He was too angry.'

'With me?' Then I took a huge intake of breath. 'You didn't tell him – Anjali, you didn't tell him about me, that both of us – you did, didn't you.'

'It just came out.'

'Oh, no. It'll be all over the compound.'

'He won't say anything. How can he? It would all come out about me as well. He won't say anything. He's a good man. He's my best friend.'

On top of everything else, this felt like a rebuke. How can you have a man as a best friend? Here I was, sharing everything with her, only to be told that there was another who meant more. I turned towards the road and there, staring at us, were three children who giggled when I looked at them.

'Get out of here,' Anjali shouted at them and they took a few steps away and continued staring. A young woman carrying a huge bundle of twigs on her head stopped as well and watched us with interest.

'Why doesn't he marry you, then?'

'Don't be stupid. How can he marry me.'

'He could, if he wanted to.'

She stared angrily out at the river.

'Hello!' Dad's voice said. I looked up and he was on the

verandah looking a little dishevelled from his sleep. 'Would you like some tea?' he asked.

'In a minute.'

'I see Mum coming. I'll put the kettle on.' He went in.

'I'd better go,' Anjali said. She got up with a sigh.

'I'll take Lucky tomorrow,' I said. 'Can I have her for the day?'

'The whole day?' Anjali asked, her face brightening.

'Yes, the whole day.'

'OK. But bring her back as soon as she's any trouble.'

'She won't be. Really. She's a lovely little girl.'

Anjali looked at me with suspicion. 'Yes,' she said shortly and turned away.

I waited for Mum. 'Hello,' she said with surprise. 'I've never sat here before.'

'It's nice, isn't it?'

'I just passed Anjali. Were you sitting here with her?'

'For a few minutes. She had to go and help Shani.'

The children and the woman were still there and they had been joined by an older man with a long solemn face.

'Perhaps we'd better go in,' I said. But Mum sat where she was, looking at the view.

'Poor Anjali,' she said. 'I do feel for her, so much. But when you get married, you've got to stick to your husband.'

'Why?'

She thought about this for a moment. 'You just do,' she said crossly. We got up and as we went up the stairs to the flat, she said, 'There's so many other people to think about, that's why. There's Roshan and Shani and little Lucky, and there's Anukal and his wife and family and there's her husband and his family.'

We stood at the door, waiting for Dad to answer the bell.

'I said I'd have Lucky for the whole day tomorrow,' I said. 'What'll you do with her?'

'Take her out to the bazaar, buy her a toy, some sweeties, that kind of thing. Will you come with us?'

'No,' Mum said, with no explanation.

156

I bought her a plastic doll and she wanted a clay one. I bought her a shiny red tin car and she whined for a green one. I bought her some sweets and she wanted more. Nothing satisfied her. The more I gave, the more dissatisfied she became. I brought her back, crying. The rickshaw man laughed.

'Do you want me to send you home?' I asked angrily.

'No, Auntie,' she sobbed.

I went to Mum in exasperation.

'She doesn't understand,' Mum said

'What?'

'Anything.'

'Neither do I.'

'Come and show me what you bought,' she said to Lucky.

But the girl wasn't interested in her toys. She wandered around the flat, looking for things to do.

'I've got to go out and see Mrs Kershaw and Morag about the Christmas party for the servants' children,' Mum said. 'Will you be all right? Shani's not here either.'

'I'll be fine,' I said, feeling relieved to be on my own with her.

'Now,' I said to Lucky, pulling her into my bedroom. 'We're going to stay in this room. No wandering about.' I rummaged around in the bottom of the wardrobe and found an old cardboard box with bits of material left over from Mum's sewing.

'Bring your doll,' I commanded the child.

She brought it obediently. I emptied the box on to the floor and watched with mounting fury as she picked up each little piece and put them back in the box. She placed the doll on her lap and delicately picked through the box, choosing pieces of cloth. She wrapped the doll in the cloth, telling it off or praising it, depending on what material she had wrapped it in. I helped her from time to time, giving her safety pins.

'This one, Auntie. Take this off and put this one on.' I showed her how to work the safety pins and she sat on the floor with her back to me and carefully pinned on cloth, her back bent over her task. The sun shone through the window and lit up her little head, her hair oiled and smelling of coconut, carefully plaited for this big day. I felt I could have sat like this for hours.

Mum returned and sat on the bed. 'Would you like a little girl?' she asked.

'I guess so. I don't know,' I said.

'One day you will, I'm sure you will. Where shall we give her lunch? She might feel a bit awkward having it with us at the big table. I thought to bring a tray through here for the two of you.'

'That's a good idea. She'll make an awful mess, I know she will.'

Lucky looked up at us, aware of being talked about.

'Are you hungry?' I asked. 'Shall we have lunch now?'

She nodded eagerly.

She sat cross-legged on the floor and ate her lunch with no mess. She ate with neat wee fingers, mixing up the rice and curry before starting and leaning over the plate as she ate. She ate a tiny amount and I tried to cajole her into eating more. 'No,' she said. 'My stomach's full.' She licked her fingers and her palm and then she held her hand out for it to be washed. I went to the bathroom and brought out a damp flannel and carefully wiped her hand and then her face, feeling clumsy and unfamiliar with this kind of thing. She smiled shyly at me, as if recognising my unfamiliarity. Then she remembered the bathroom.

'I need to do pee pee,' she said, her eyes glittering. I laughed.

The afternoon slipped by easily. While Mum and Dad had their rest, I found myself telling stories to her. This was something else I was unfamiliar with but I knew it was what you did with children. Her eyes were fixed on my face, utterly fascinated.

'Tell me that one again, Auntie,' she said, so I told her again about the little girl in Edinburgh Castle who alerted the guards to an attack by the English. I told her about the dark clouds and the cold and the silent night, and the men below climbing up the rocks.

'Again, Auntie.'

'No, I'll tell you another one.' I told her about Robert the Bruce hiding after the battle with the English and seeing the spider in the cave. She wanted to hear about the battle and the horses and the swords.

'What happened to the king?' she asked.

'He died an old man.'

She was disappointed. I told her about Bonny Prince Charlie and the Highlanders fighting the English and how they marched for a whole day and all they had to eat was a handful of rice. Then I ran out of battles and returned to the girl in Edinburgh Castle.

'You look happy,' Mum said, when I came back from taking her home.

'I'm utterly exhausted.'

'Your eyes are shining and happy,' she said, looking at me and smiling but a little apprehensive as if wondering what was going to happen next. 'Children do that to you,' she said.

'Make you exhausted?'

'Make you happy.'

22

WHILE DAD SAID GRACE, I imagined Rahul and Paul with huge erections under the table. Paul's was clothed in rubber but Rahul's was glisteningly brown and naked.

Drums approached from a distance as we were eating.

'Who's getting married?' I asked.

'No, no,' Rahul said. 'It is Ganesh puja. They are bringing the idol to the river.

'Here?' Dad asked sharply.

'Must be. These steps, you know – ?'

'No,' Dad said, angrily shaking his head. 'I don't know.' He gave Rahul a fierce look with his grey eyes.

Paul glanced around expectantly. Dad put his fork down and went to the front verandah.

'Where is he going?' Mrs Sen asked.

'I have no idea,' Mum said.

'The river front is college property,' Mr Sen said quietly. 'Technically, there should be no Hindu ceremonies on it.' He took a mouthful of rice and curry and turned to watch Dad as he chewed.

I joined Dad. He was standing with his arms stretched tight and his hands pressed on the railing. He watched the crowd below as they lifted the idol down from people's shoulders and placed it under the tree by the steps. A priest stepped forward and began chanting and spraying the idol with rose water. People milled around excitedly.

He turned and went back in to the room and spoke to Mr Sen. 'That river side is college property,' he said.

'That is so,' Mr Sen agreed.

'They shouldn't be performing a Hindu ceremony on Christian land,' Dad said.

He looked insistently at Mr Sen who avoided his eyes and glanced at his wife who ate on, unperturbed.

'What can we do?' he said. 'Let the fellows have their puja and I'll speak to someone in the morning.'

Dad hesitated.

'My friend, the Superintendent of police –,' Mr Sen began.

'It'll be too late then,' Dad said.

'Please sit down, David,' Mum said. 'This is nothing to do with you.'

'This is everything to do with me,' he insisted angrily.

'No, it isn't,' she said. 'Please sit down.' Mrs Sen put down her fork.

'I'm going to stop them,' he said and walked with long strides to the door.

We let him go alone.

Paul got up and went to the verandah and we all followed him. I didn't like the way he was enjoying this excitement. Roshan came and stood beside me. 'What's going on?' he asked me quietly.

'Dad says this is Christian ground and they shouldn't be doing their puja on it. He's going to ask them to go.'

'These Bengalis, they're too excitable,' he said, leaning over the railings.

'He really shouldn't be doing this,' Mr Sen said.

'Anything could happen,' Paul said with relish.

'I'll go down,' Rahul said and hurried away.

I saw Dad's head, tall above the small Bengalis, talking and insisting, pointing with his long arm to the river and then away from it and then pointing at the ground. The crowd had stilled and were talking to each other. What's going on? they were saying, pressing up close to hear.

He pushed his way through the crowd towards the idol. It

161

was Ganesh, the little god that I had always liked with the fat complacent body and the elephant's head, as if it were the most natural thing in the world to have such a head and four little white hands delicately spread. People were trying to lift the idol and carry it to the river, but Dad went up to it and gave it a push, struggling to keep it from the river. I watched exultantly as the crowd surged forward angrily, shouting now. Yes, that's right. Shove him away. Who the hell does he think he is?

'David!' Mum cried.

He disappeared under the weight of the angry people. Some turned towards us and waved their fists and pointed and began shouting up at the verandah. All the servants had come out of their houses and were watching in wonder.

'Eh, Lalu!' Mr Sen shouted down. Ganga's husband looked up.

'What shall I do?' he asked.

'Run for the police,' Mr Sen commanded. 'Run, run.' Lalu looked at the gate, blocked now by the crowd.

'The back way, man, the back way. Climb over the wall!' Lalu ran behind the flats.

'Where is he? Can you see him?' Paul asked. 'Isabel, can you see him?'

'I see Rahul,' Mrs Sen said. 'Oh, my God.'

Rahul was fighting his way through with Roshan behind him. I hadn't noticed him go.

'What's going on?' Keislar asked, suddenly beside me. He ducked as a stone flew past him.

'Come inside!' Mrs Sen cried in fear.

Mum ignored the stones that were bouncing off the netting. I crawled over to her. 'Where is he? Stupid, stupid man,' she said.

'Get down, Mum.' She crouched down and we peered through the railings.

Rahul and Roshan pulled Dad through the angry people and they climbed over the gate. The men on this side helped him down. Now everybody was throwing stones and shouting. We crawled inside and watched from the window. The servants had

162

run away and the crowd was pressed up against the gate. Any minute now they'd open it.

Dad came in. 'I'm all right,' he said irritably, pushing Mum away. He was very pale. His arms hung by his side and his hands trembled. People stood in a circle around him, wondering what to do with him.

'Don't get angry with me,' Mum shouted. 'Look what you've done!'

'We must keep calm,' Mr Sen said. 'I've sent Lalu for the police.'

'Was that necessary?' Dad asked.

We waited, expecting the anger to die down. Fewer stones were thrown but suddenly the shouting became shrill. The police had come. They were beating the crowd with huge sticks. People ran up and down the road, trying to get away.

'Oh, God,' Mum cried. 'What are they doing to the people.'

There were voices out on the landing and a banging on the door. Roshan went towards it and then looked at Dad.

'Ask who it is,' Dad said.

It was two policemen and the priest. The priest was a small fat man in a dhoti, with orange marking smeared across his forehead. He looked subdued standing between the two policemen. One of the policemen, an officer, sat down on the wooden sofa and leaned back, taking a good look around him.

'You have not finished your meal,' he said in English. No one replied. 'Which Sahib was it?' he asked the priest. The man pointed at Dad. 'He says you kicked the idol.'

'I did no such thing,' Dad said.

'He insists that you did. That was why they started rioting.' He had a handsome, petulant face.

'I told them that where they were going to perform their puja was college property.'

'So? Prayers cannot be said on college property? Do you not say them yourselves?'

'It is Christian ground,' Dad said. 'I tried to explain that we could not allow a Hindu ceremony to take place on Christian ground.'

'You were upset.'

'No, I was quite firm.' But his hands were still trembling. The policeman looked pointedly at them.

'There are numerous people who say they saw you kick the idol,' he said.

'We did not see such a thing,' Keislar said. 'We were standing out there the whole time. Until they started throwing stones.'

The policeman got up slowly and went to the verandah door. Rahul opened the shutters for him and he went outside. Then he came back in to the room. 'It is very dark down there,' he said. 'And with a large crowd. What could you see?' he asked Keislar. 'Could you see feet?'

Keislar hesitated. 'No,' he admitted. 'But it is not a thing Mr Walker would do.'

No, everybody said. It was not a thing he would do. Dad remained silent.

'I am sorry, sir, but I am having to arrest you for inciting a riot. You will come with us, please, now, sir.'

The other policeman went over to Dad.

'This is not right,' Mr Sen said. 'The Superintendent is known to me. I will protest to him. This is not right.'

The policeman looked at me and then at Mum. 'This is her father?' he asked her.

'Yes,' I said, trying to sound cold and decisive.

'Don't be frightened,' he said, smiling condescendingly. 'You must not be afraid.'

'I'm not.'

He indicated to Dad that they should go and Rahul said, 'I'll come with you.'

'I will come also,' Mr Sen said.

'David!' Mum cried, going towards him. He motioned to her with a fluttering hand. It could have meant come to me, or stay where you are. She stood with her hands on her cheeks as they left.

'I will remain,' Mrs Sen said and sat down.

Mum and I ran to the verandah and watched as the men

walked through the crowd of servants to the compound gate. Dogs roamed about, barking.

'What's happening, Memsahib?' Ganga asked. 'Where are they going?'

'They've arrested him,' Mum said with tears in her voice.

There were cries of alarm and dismay. Anjali came running through the gate. 'What's going on?' she called up to me. 'Where's he going?'

They've arrested him, everyone told her. There was a riot and they've taken the Sahib away. She came up the stairs and into the flat. Ganga and Jamuna and Lalu came up with her, along with several children. Servants from the other compound came in too and stood around the walls, shy but eager for excitement. Padma was there and I was glad to see her. She stood across from Mum and covered her head with her sari.

'Why have they arrested him, Hannah?' Anjali asked. The room stilled, waiting for my reply.

'They say he kicked the idol and started the riot,' I said. My own hands were shaking and my voice trembled slightly.

People looked at one another, doubtful and amazed.

'Memsahib,' Ganga said. 'He wouldn't do such a thing. He's a good man, a beautiful man. Why would he do such a thing. They're lying.'

Yes, people solemnly agreed. He was a good man, a beautiful man. Mum sat in a chair, looking distracted.

'But why did they start throwing stones?' Jamuna asked. 'Why did he go down there?'

I explained, and people murmured to each other. I didn't know that. Did you know that? I didn't know that. I thought it was part of the road. I thought it belonged to everybody. They shifted uncomfortably, not knowing which side to take. Keislar and Paul sat on the dining-room chairs, talking quietly to one another. Mrs Sen sat beside Mum on the couch. The children looked around the room with large eyes.

'Of course it's Christian land,' Padma said. 'Isn't this a Christian College? Well, isn't it?'

'But it's outside the gate,' a man said.

'Don't you worry, Memsahib,' she said loudly, ignoring the man. 'They'll soon see they've made a mistake. He'll be back tomorrow. These police people, they're such fools.'

There was agreement with this. Anjali put her arm around my waist and looked up at me with a worried face. Ganga looked at me too. Then she put her old hand lightly on Mum's shoulder. 'He'll be back tomorrow, Memsahib. You'll see,' she said quietly.

'Thank you,' Mum said, holding her hand.

Lalu said, 'Come on, we'll go now.'

Roshan stood beside the dining-room table with his hands behind his back, watching as the people left slowly. Children turned around for a last look.

'Shani's with Lucky,' Anjali said. 'Lucky's got a fever so Shani stayed with her. But I know she wants to be with you, Memsahib. When I get back I'll send her over.'

'That's all right,' Mum said. 'I've got Hannah with me. You and Shani stay with Lucky. I hope she gets better. Do you need any medicine?'

'We've got some, Memsahib. It's not too bad, just a small fever.'

'But best to keep an eye on it,' Mum said.

'Yes, we're doing that.'

When they had left Roshan cleared his throat. 'It's gone cold,' he said, indicating the table. 'Shall I heat something up for you?'

'Do you want anything, Hannah? I'm not hungry.'

'Me neither.'

'I should have offered it to them,' Mum said, looking at the door. 'What a lot it must have looked to them.'

'Put it away until tomorrow,' Mrs Sen ordered Roshan. He hesitated and when Mum said nothing he began clearing the table. Keislar and Paul stood up and hovered around Mum.

'I will wait with her,' Mrs Sen said.

I wanted them all to go. They stood where they were.

'Go, go,' Mrs Sen commanded.

'You'll knock if you need anything,' Paul said. 'Any time of the night, it doesn't matter.'

'I will,' Mum said. 'Thank you.' They left reluctantly.

'I would like to be alone with my mother,' I said.

Mrs Sen looked at me as if to say, oh, it's you, but she didn't move. 'Please,' I said.

'She needs an older woman with her, not a chit of a girl.'

'I'm not a chit of a girl. You've been very kind but I want to be alone with her.'

The woman shifted in her chair and adjusted her sari around her legs and then looked at Mum. 'I will stay,' she said, but Mum got up and went to the verandah door and stood with her back to us. I stayed beside Mrs Sen like a barrier and the woman heaved herself up from the sofa. 'A shocking night,' she said. 'Shocking. Your mother is very frightened. You take care of her like a good daughter. I will go home and wait for my husband. We will see what tomorrow brings.'

She left without saying goodbye to Mum, just looking curiously at her withdrawn back.

Roshan cleared his throat. 'Memsahib,' he said. Mum turned to him. 'Shall I ask Shani to come?' He was gruffly gentle. He had never spoken to her like this before. There was usually a bit of hostility between them, as if they could never work out once and for all who was the boss.

'No,' she said. 'Not tonight. Lucky's got a fever.'

'I'll go then,' he said.

'Yes.'

After he had gone I cleared my throat to see the effect of breaking the silence.

'Why would they say something like that if he hadn't done it?'

'It's not like him to do that.'

'I think it is. I think he did it.'

We stared at this vision of Dad, as if we had never seen him before. Working steadily and quietly in his sternness and goodness, we had no idea what kind of thoughts he'd been having all this time.

'Do you know what his one piece of advice to me was when I left for university?' I asked.

'No. What?'

'That when I shared digs, to always clean the bath after me. I always did.'

'I can't remember what I said to you. Probably a lot of nonsense.'

'Probably.'

She came and sat down on the edge of her chair in the sitting-room. She leaned over her lap, clutching her arms and looking at the floor.

'I should have kept my unhappiness to myself. I shouldn't have pushed it all onto him.'

'This isn't your fault, Mum. This is all his doing. You know what he's like, with that ferocious integrity of his.'

'Don't I just.' She sighed and stood up. 'I'll make some coffee. Do you want some?'

'Yes, please.' I followed her to the kitchen and we stopped at the door while Mum reached in and put on the light. Cockroaches scuttled in all directions. We waited silently until it was clear.

She filled a battered old kettle and put it on the stove.

'I didn't feed the dogs this evening. I think I'll do it now.' She got out three bowls and went to the fridge, looked in for a long moment and then closed it. She broke bread and poured milk over it. Going quickly to the fridge again, she got out pieces of meat from the uneaten curry and distributed them carefully between each bowl. She picked up two bowls. She hesitated and I took the third one and we went downstairs.

A third dog had arrived to take Sheraphuli's place, a thin brown and black dog with a long sharp muzzle. Not a bitch, I noticed with relief.

'What are you going to call it, Memsahib?'. Ganga asked, coming out of her door.

'I don't know yet. I'll think of a name.'

'Yes, you think of one. It's a quiet dog. Not like this one that barks all night,' she said, pointing to Hugh. Some people drifted over to watch the feeding and stood with their hands behind their backs, expectant but quiet even though I could see that they wanted to talk.

'How are you now, Memsahib?' Jamuna asked.

'I'm all right, thank you.'

'That's good.' Her eyes were greedy for more and she caught my eye and smiled.

As we went upstairs, Mum asked, 'Do you think they saw the meat?'

'It was too dark. And the dogs ate it too quickly.'

'What shall we do now?'

'I don't know.'

We returned to our seats in the sitting-room.

'The coffee!' Mum said and got up to make it.

As we drank it Mum said in a heavy voice, 'I wonder what he's doing now.'

We waited for two hours and then Rahul returned. We stood nervously, waiting for him to speak. He looked tired and upset.

'He's being kept overnight,' he said, glancing at the floor and then at Mum's hands.

'Where?'

'At the prison.'

'Oh,' Mum cried. 'Why?'

'Until Mr Sen can raise bail.'

'What's the prison like?' I asked.

He raised his hands and then dropped them, looking uneasily at me.

'And they will let him out tomorrow?' Mum asked.

'That's what they say. But who knows? Mr Sen sends all his reassurances and says not to worry, he will be home with you tomorrow.'

'Do you think he will?' Mum asked him quite firmly, wanting the truth.

'Who knows. But that is a small matter, surely. What we have to think about now is what comes next.'

We looked at this silently.

'I'm tired,' Rahul said. 'I'm going home now.' His eyes darted to each of us and then he left.

'He's very upset,' I said.

'Yes, very.'

He seemed more upset than we were.

23

ROSHAN SERVED US BREAKFAST gravely the next morning. We told him what Rahul had said.

'Prison,' he said angrily, and jerked his chin towards the verandah door. 'It's they who should be in prison.'

When we had finished, Roshan cleared the table but we sat on. 'It's so quiet without him,' Mum said. 'You wouldn't think so, him being such a quiet man and in his study all the time.'

It was true. The place rang with emptiness.

Shani arrived early. 'Memsahib,' she said, with tears in her eyes. Mum stood up and put out her arms and hugged her friend. 'We must pray, Memsahib. We must pray for him, that they let him go. God won't let anything happen to him, you'll see.'

'How is Lucky?' Mum asked.

'She's much better. The temperature has come right down. It was just a small thing, thank God.'

'That's good,' Mum said.

Shani began her work with her long thin face looking concentrated and unhappy.

Mrs Kershaw was the first to come. 'Oh, Isabel,' she said, clasping her podgy hands over her stomach as she sat down with us at the table. 'What can I do for you? Does he have a lawyer?'

Mum and I looked at each other. We hadn't thought of a lawyer. 'I wonder if Mr Sen is seeing to that,' Mum said. 'I should go over and see him.'

'He's gone back to the police station. Mrs Sen came down as we were having breakfast. He's such a fierce man, she kept saying. Such a fierce man. I've always thought of him as a very gentle man. What is he, Hannah? What's your father like? Fierce or gentle?'

'That's because he told her off once,' Mum said.

'Told her off?' I asked in delight.

'I didn't know where to look,' Mum said. 'But she's been terribly meek towards him ever since. Yes, Dr Walker, No, Dr Walker.'

'I wish I'd seen that,' I said.

Mrs Kershaw gave a shrill little laugh and then there was a silence between us, companionable. Mum fiddled with a tea spoon.

'Shall we do the accounts, Memsahib?' Roshan asked.

'Not today,' Mum said. 'I'll give you ten rupees and you just buy what you want.' She got up and fetched the money from a secret file in one of Dad's filing cabinets that they disguised by labelling 'filthy lucre'. 'Will that be enough?' she asked.

'Yes, enough, Memsahib,' he said, and left for the bazaar.

The doorbell rang and I answered it. It was Keislar, looking concerned. 'Any news?' he asked.

'No, not yet.'

'Call me when you have some,' he said. 'I'm going over to see Mr Sen now. I'll come back and let you know what he says.'

'All right.'

'This is a terrible business.'

'Yes, it is.'

'Tell your mother I'll be back soon with some news.'

'Yes, I'll do that.'

He left with a nod, a man with a mission.

When I came back into the room, Mum was sitting with her hand on her chin, looking out of the verandah door and humming Lille Marlene. She had a record of Marlene Dietrich singing this but her voice had none of the husky sexiness of Marlene's. Instead, in her high soprano, she was humming it for the sake of the lovely lilt of the tune, bringing out the

172

sadness. Mrs Kershaw began to hum along with her. Her's was a richer soprano and she quickened the tempo, making it into a march. The bell rang again and I went reluctantly to the door. It was Morag, clutching another white fluffy dog. Hearing the singing, she looked over my shoulder in surprise and I led her into the room.

'You guys,' she said, smiling. Then she joined in, standing beside Mrs Kershaw, earnestly singing in German, carefully enunciating each resonant, foreign word. Shani stood at the door with a brush in her hand, smiling, her eyes going from woman to woman. We came to the end and burst out laughing.

'What do the words mean?' I asked Morag. Morag looked puzzled.

'I don't know,' she confessed and pulled up a chair and sat down with the dog in her lap. Mrs Kershaw looked at it.

'I take him everywhere with me,' Morag said.

Mrs Sen was the next to arrive. She settled herself comfortably on the sofa and beckoned to Shani. 'Go and buy me some peanuts,' she said, handing her a rupee note. Shani looked at the note and took it with distaste, unable to refuse.

'This dog,' Mrs Sen said, indicating it with her head. 'I thought it was dead.'

'I got another one,' Morag said.

'You like this kind of dog?'

'Yes, I like it very much. Do you like dogs?' she asked nervously.

'You see, I don't understand why people love animals so much. So messy and dirty.' She looked at Mrs Kershaw and smiled as to someone who would agree with her. 'They can't talk. What do they do?'

'They're always there,' Mrs Kershaw said.

'Exactly. They are always there,' Mrs Sen said.

'I mean, whatever happens, they're there as a friend,' Mrs Kershaw said.

Mrs Sen examined this extraordinary statement. 'You have no friends? Me, I have plenty. I like a friend who can talk back to me.' And she gave a little bark of a laugh.

'It's hard to make friends here,' Mum said.

'Yes, it is,' Mrs Kershaw quickly agreed.

'I thought it was just me,' Morag said. 'I guess it takes a while. Did it take a while for you guys? I've never been able to ask that. Charlie says it takes a while. You know –,' But she changed her mind.

'What?' Mum asked gently.

'Well, we ain't been married that long and, well . . . .' She leaned over and patted the dog.

'Yes, I know,' Mum said.

'And how,' Mrs Kershaw said, and laughed.

Mrs Sen looked on, gathering secrets.

Shani returned and dropped a large bag made out of newspapers beside Mrs Sen.

'Make some tea,' Mrs Sen ordered and Shani went into the kitchen. Mum went in with her and they murmured softly to each other. Mrs Sen began cracking the shells. 'Come, come,' she said to me, waving to the bag. I got up from the table and took a handful and sat down in Dad's chair. Morag and Mrs Kershaw got up too and helped themselves and sat in the sitting-room. I was surprised to see how skilful Morag was at opening the peanuts and she ate them delicately, putting the shells in a careful pile in her lap. Mrs Sen cracked them with gusto, gathered the opened ones in her palm, rubbed them with her fingers, blew away the papery under-skins and tossed them into her mouth.

'I haven't had peanuts for ages,' Mrs Kershaw said.

'We eat them all the time at home,' Morag said.

'You have peanuts in America?' Mrs Sen asked, chewing.

'We grow them. I didn't know there were peanuts in India. I always thought of them as being an American thing. You know, peanut-butter?' There was a note of longing in her voice.

Mrs Sen cracked another nut. The floor was a mess of peanut shells and skins.

Mum and Shani handed round tea.

'You're very pale, Hannah,' Mrs Kershaw said.

'Poor girl, worried for her father,' Mrs Sen said. 'Go lie down. Go, go.' She pointed to the door.

'No, I'm OK.'

'I find a prayer helps in a time like this,' Mrs Kershaw said, looking at me. God, did she expect me to say one?

'Or reading the Bible,' Morag said, also looking at me. 'What's your favourite story?'

I had neither prayed nor picked up the Bible since I was about ten. The only story I could remember was Lot's wife turning to salt. 'I haven't a favourite,' I said.

'Mine's the book of Ruth,' Mrs Kershaw said.

'I like that one too,' Mum said.

Mrs Kershaw gave her brief laugh. Then she clasped her hands and sighed. 'A hard act to follow.'

Mrs Sen cracked a nut.

'Why?' I asked.

'Don't you know it?' Mrs Kershaw said. 'It's the one where Ruth's husband dies and she follows her mother-in-law into Israel.'

'Naomi,' Mrs Sen said.

'Ruth said to Naomi, "Your people will be my people, your God my God, and where you die, there will I be buried,"' Mum said, her eyes red.

Mrs Kershaw looked at the floor. 'So much trust in one person – and in God too – that she followed her into a strange country.'

'And love,' Mum said. 'She must have loved her very much.'

'Mine is Daniel,' Morag said. '"Now let Daniel be called". I kinda like that even though I don't know why.' She gave a little giggle and then picked the dog up and put it on her lap.

'In the lion's den,' Mrs Sen said. 'Very fine.'

There was the sound of feet outside the door and male voices talking low. The bell rang and everyone looked at Mum. She stiffened, put her hands on the arms of her chair as if to rise and then tilted her head back in a gesture of alarm that irritated me with its theatricality.

'I'll go,' I said, jumping up.

175

24

DAD STOOD THERE WITH Mr Sen and Rahul. When they came in everyone stood. Dad looked pale and tired, his tall body stooped. He stood behind a chair and put one hand on it for support, his eyes shifting around the people, unsmiling.

'Sit down,' Rahul entreated.

'I'm fine,' he said crossly.

'You see – we've brought him back to you,' Mr Sen said to Mum. There was a half hearted attempt at a flourish in his manner.

Mrs Kershaw and Morag gathered themselves up and left, pausing at Dad's side to tell him how glad they were to see him.

'Yes,' he said, shortly. 'Thank you.'

Rahul and Mr and Mrs Sen remained, hovering around Dad. Shani was quickly sweeping up the peanut shells and Dad watched her as she did so.

'It's all over now,' Rahul said quietly to Mum.

'All over?' she asked, looking at Dad.

'Yes, finished and done with,' Mr Sen said, but there was a reluctance in his voice to explain.

Dad continued looking at Shani and when she finished his eyes followed her back as she went to the kitchen.

'We'll leave you now,' Mr Sen said. 'Plenty to talk about, eh? But this episode is just that, just an episode and now it is finished. Life goes on, does it not, Isabel?'

'I don't know,' she said.

'Of course it does,' Mr Sen said briskly, and he and his wife and Rahul left.

'Shall we sit down?' I asked awkwardly, feeling like a hostess.

Mum went over to Dad. He fumbled for her hand and pressed it and then let it go.

'Shall I make some tea?' I asked.

There was the sound of the key in the door and Roshan came into the flat. His face lit up when he saw Dad. He came over to him and salaamed him with a serious face. Dad returned the salaam.

'Thank you for what you did,' he said.

'You're safe now,' Roshan said.

'Thank you very much,' Dad said.

Roshan went into the kitchen where he and Shani spoke quietly to each other.

'Well, perhaps we should sit down,' Dad said and went over to his chair and lowered himself into it slowly.

'I'll make tea,' Mum said, and I was left alone with Dad.

'Are you hungry?' I asked.

'No,' he said.

'We've been eating peanuts.'

'And making a terrible mess,' Dad said, looking at the clean floor.

'What are servants for, after all?'

He laughed stiffly. We both glanced towards the kitchen. Then Mum joined us.

'Roshan will bring the tea when it's ready. He wants to know if you want anything to eat. He can make something quickly. Or would you like toast? he says.'

'No, nothing, thank you.'

Mum sat in her chair and leaned forward.

'Well,' Dad began, crossing his legs and looking at the wall opposite. 'It was pretty awful, as you can imagine, but the people couldn't have been nicer.'

'What people?' I asked.

'The other prisoners,' he said.

'What about the police?' Mum asked. 'What were they like?'

'Just doing their job. One or two were a bit short with me.'

'In what way?' I asked.

'A bit rough. But then that's all part of their work.' He looked down at his hands.

'But the prisoners were kind,' Mum said.

'Oh, very. Brought me tea, showed me where to sleep, that kind of thing.'

'I don't suppose you slept much,' I said.

'No.'

'What did Mr Sen mean when he said it's all over now?' Mum asked, looking at him anxiously. 'Did they drop the charges?'

'Not exactly. We had to pay them some money.'

'Who? Who did you pay?'

'The police,' he said shortly, irritated again.

'You bribed them, Dad?'

'Well, yes. Yes, you could call it that.'

'What would you call it?' Mum asked.

He waved a hand in the air but didn't reply. Roshan came in with a tray and placed it carefully on the small table beside Dad's chair. There was a pot of tea, a cup and saucer and a pile of toast wrapped up in a napkin to keep warm.

'Thank you,' Dad said to him, and poured himself a cup. The teapot shook as he poured. I looked away. I turned back when I heard him buttering a slice of toast.

'What would have happened if you hadn't?' I asked.

'We would have been deported,' Mum said at once.

'Yes, there's no question of that,' Dad said, looking at her and then taking a bite of his toast. He ate all the pieces of toast, bite by meticulous bite, and Roshan looked pleased when he came to take the tray away and saw the empty plate.

'How much?' Mum asked as he was eating.

'A thousand rupees,' he said with his mouth full of toast.

'Is that a lot or a little for a bribe?' I asked.

'I don't know,' he said. 'Mr Sen and Rahul seemed to think it the right amount.'

'But where's it coming from?' I asked.

'I'll have to send home for some,' he said, glancing at Mum. They had a little private capital.

'Whose idea was it?' I asked.

'Well, it just arose. Nobody's in particular. I can't remember who said it first.' He poured himself another cup, his hand steadier now.

'And they let you go without any actual cash in their hands?' I said.

'They knew they could rely on me.'

'They ken where your bairns go to school,' I said.

He took a few sips of tea and then carefully put the cup back on the saucer. 'I think I'll go and lie down for an hour or so.'

Mum remained sitting as she was, leaning over her lap, looking at the floor.

Feeling that one of us should express some kind of welcome to him, I said, 'It's nice to have you back, Dad.'

'Well, it's nice to be back.' He looked at Mum and then went to the bedroom, shutting the door quietly behind him. When the door clicked shut, Mum straightened her back.

'Well,' I said.

'It's time we were getting ready for Christmas,' Mum said, looking towards the kitchen and putting her hands on the arms of her chair, as if to rise.

'Where are you going?'

'To make a list for Christmas.' But she didn't get up. She leaned forward in her chair again, and looked at the grey cement floor to the side of her. 'I really thought we'd be deported and I'd get home. I guess it was wrong to think like that. That's no answer.' She sighed. 'I've got to be more trusting like Ruth.'

'With Dad as Naomi, you mean?' I said dryly.

'It would have been terrible for her, with her husband dead, left alone with no money. I sometimes think of Naomi and wonder what kind of woman she was.'

'Pretty tough, I should think.'

'She sent Ruth to lie at the feet of Boaz. I don't think I could do that to you,' Mum said. 'I wish I could.'

'What, send me to have sex with someone?' I was astonished.

179

'No, no,' she said and looked at the floor. Her cheeks were flushed. 'But whose feet would you want to lie at?' she asked, looking at me again, her face serious and intent. 'How about Rahul's? It would be nice if you married Rahul. There you would be, just across the compound.'

'But that's what some people do. They marry the man down the road and live within shouting distance of their mothers. That seems so strange. Marriage is about going away.'

'Why not Rahul?' she asked. 'Why not him? He's very nice.'

'Men don't seem to want me. Not for marriage anyway.'

'Has nobody asked you?'

Dad's bed creaked as he got into it.

'No,' I admitted.

'Well, you ask them then. You go and ask Rahul to marry you.'

'But I don't want to marry him, Mum. I can't imagine being married to anyone.'

'Don't you want to be married?'

The hard leaves of the almond tree scraped against one another.

'I guess I do.'

'Sometimes I wish I wasn't. But then if I hadn't married, I wouldn't have had you. It's children who matter, not husbands.'

'You don't have to be married to have children,' I said quietly. Dad's bed creaked again.

'No,' Mum said. 'But it can't be easy.'

'Anjali seems to manage,' I said.

'I don't think she's very happy.'

Hugh gave a few barks and from the other compound another dog barked back. Jamuna called out to somebody and the gate banged shut as she closed it behind her.

'No,' I said. 'But then, who is?'

She stood up and got her bag that was lying on the table. She took out a little notebook and sat down again. I watched her, the breath tight in my chest.

'I'll make a list for Christmas,' Mum said. 'What would you

180

like for a present? I suppose you'll be going back soon after Christmas. In time for the new term.'

I didn't reply.

She fiddled with her pen and wrote a couple of things. She fiddled again.

'Why don't you ask Rahul what he saw?' she asked, looking at her notebook.

'You mean, if he saw Dad kick the idol?'

'Yes.'

'I could ask him, I suppose.'

'Yes, why not.'

'But you must ask Dad too.'

'Yes, yes, I'll do that. I'll ask him.'

'Do you think he did kick the idol?'

'Ask Rahul,' she said lightly.

It was like a game we were playing. We stopped suddenly and there was a silence.

'I don't think you should ask him,' I said, imagining his face pale and angry and his eyes shifting guiltily.

'No, I will. Why shouldn't I?' She bent over her list. 'Let's buy him some whisky from the foreign liquor store.'

'Good idea.'

She carefully wrote whisky at the top of her list.

25

DAD SLEPT THROUGH LUNCH. After we had eaten I got up from the table.

'I'll go and see Rahul now.'

'You do that,' Mum said but with a false conviction in her voice. We paused awkwardly, avoiding each other's eyes.

I walked over slowly and self-consciously, swinging my hips, in the way Indian women walk, stately and graciously, as if they knew exactly where they were going. I went up the stairs and knocked on his door. A few students watched me curiously as I stood on the verandah waiting for him to answer.

'I didn't get you out of bed, I hope,' I said when he opened the door.

'Not this time,' he answered and stood aside to let me in. 'You've eaten?'

'Yes.'

'I'm just returning from the dining-room. Everyone's talking about your father.'

'What do they say?'

'They want to know exactly what happened, all the details, even what we were eating for dinner, and especially what Mrs Sen was doing all the while. I tell them everything except about Mrs Sen. I don't remember what she said.'

'Neither do I.'

'For such a big mouth, she was very quiet.' He sat me down as he talked and sat down himself opposite me with the table

182

between us, as before. His eyes were bright with excitement, eager, I could see, to go over the details once more. His eyes didn't dart about but fixed themselves on me.

'How is your father?'

'Very tired. He was sleeping when I left. Thank you for what you did.'

He looked down at his hand resting on the table. 'What did I do?' he asked quietly.

'The way you brought him back. I don't know what would have happened otherwise.'

'He's a man with a strong mind. Very determined.'

'You were very brave.'

He waved his hand in the air as if chasing away a fly. 'Oh, brave,' he said but he looked pleased. 'You want tea?' he asked, standing up. 'I'll make tea.'

He went into his little kitchen and I followed him, watching as he filled a battered dekchi with water and put it on an electric ring, turning the ring on to full. He took a brown paper bag down from a shelf and spooned in two heaps of tealeaves and from another bag poured in a little trickle of sugar. He paused and looked vaguely around him and then picked up an enamel cup from the rickety table and poured in some milk from it. There was a teaspoon in the heavy stone sink and he ran some water over it from the tap and gave the mixture a slow stir. The kitchen smelled musty and unused but as the tea heated up it began to smell sweet and milky. I leaned against the doorway, casually.

He reached into the deep sink and rinsed out a thick white china cup and then went to a little netted cupboard and brought out another which he also rinsed, placing both on the table.

'They think he shouldn't have done it,' he said as we watched the dekchi, waiting for it to boil.

'Why not?'

'Upsetting things like that, making trouble. What did it matter, they say, one little puja. They feel quite shocked. But these fellows,' he said with a contemptuous lift of his chin. 'They are shocked too easily.'

'It's just like him to do something like that. You know, sticking to his principles.'

'Principles,' he said in his slow way and I blushed for Dad. He saw my face and smiled.

He poured out the tea and stirred it again in the cups, his fingers delicate and sure, and tossed the spoon with a clatter into the sink. Someone knocked on his door and I turned towards it but he took a sip of his hot tea and looked at the floor. They knocked again but he continued sipping.

'Come in here,' he said, going into the bedroom. 'They can't hear us in here.'

I followed him and he shut the door behind us. We stood awkwardly and then he sat on the bed. As there was no chair in the room I sat down beside him. He put his tea down on the floor and lay back, holding himself up on his elbows. I sat on the edge and sipped.

'I like this short hair,' he said.

'Oh,' I said.

He touched my back and I stiffened.

'Come,' he whispered. 'Come, come.' There was no urgency in his voice, just an unhurried cajoling. But I would rather have had urgency, not this feeling of trying things out, of fumbling in an unsure way.

I put the tea on the floor beside his and shifted beside him, leaning back on my elbows. I stared at the door, wondering what on earth I should say. We stayed like this for a horrible minute. Then he cleared his throat and I felt him shift and he touched my hand. God, this man business, this sex business, all this coming together. What's it for? I turned towards him and our eyes bounced off each other.

'Is this all right?' he asked my hand.

'Yes.' It was a dark, hot, naked little room. The day looked white and bright outside the open window.

'Do you get mosquitos here?'

'Yes,' he said.

'You haven't any netting on your window.'

He turned to look at it and then glanced at me, surprised and

184

apprehensive. I put my hand on his and immediately he stroked my face. I turned to lie on my side and he did the same. It was too late to say, thanks for the tea, I'm off now.

'You've done this before?' he whispered, playing with my fingers.

'Well, you know . . . .'

'No,' he said. 'I don't.'

I felt embarrassed for him. I was used to men who knew what they were doing. Or at least, pretending to. And Rahul lay there, not pretending anything.

'You don't mind?' I asked.

'What?'

'About me.'

'No, I don't mind.'

I took his hand and pressed it against my breast. He got up onto his knees and began unbuttoning my blouse and, poor thing, his fingers trembled. I sat up and helped him. I took my blouse off and we hesitated for a few seconds.

'You will take it off?' he said, looking at my bra.

I took it off. He stared at my breasts. Then he took a nipple experimentally between finger and thumb and I laughed. He looked a little abashed and spread his hands to engulf them but his hands weren't big enough. His brown skin made my skin look white and fragile. I looked everywhere except at his face and he pulled me closer to him and began to fondle my breasts in great earnestness, squeezing and pressing them.

'Does this hurt?' he asked, his voice quick and urgent.

'No,' I said, even though it did. I always said no. If I said yes they might get discouraged. And then that erection, which I was responsible for and which this was all about, would wither and die.

I began to unbutton his shirt, wanting to get on to the next stage. When I got to his trousers he let go of my breasts and turned his back to me and took off his shirt and trousers. I began undressing too and when he was naked he slipped quickly between the sheets while I struggled out of my jeans. All I saw was his back, bent and hurried. He got a good look at me as I got in beside him. Then we lay on the bed and he was hesitating so I leaned over and kissed his dry lips. They were puckered and hard. I licked his mouth and he turned his head away.

'This is what you do?' he asked.

'Whatever you want,' I said. But when I leaned over him he turned away again.

'What's wrong?' I asked.

'This kissing business,' he said, looking at the ceiling.

'You don't like it?'

'No, I don't like it.'

He glanced at me warily.

'Why not?' I ducked my head and began to stroke his chest, thinking I had bad breath.

'Oh,' he said. 'It is not necessary. Not for me.'

I looked down his compact little body, pale and not too hairy, which I liked. I didn't like a man looking like a monkey. His penis lay hard against his body.

I licked my way down his chest and his flat stomach, tasting salty, sweaty skin. When I came to his penis I picked it up, gagged slightly, then put it in my mouth. Once I had the gagging over, I was always fine.

'How's that?' I said, after a moment.

'Interesting.'

I laughed a little.

'I'm disappointing you, I think,' he said, his head seeming miles away.

'Am I disappointing you?'

'No, no.' His tone was polite.

'Then what? Shall I go on?'

'There is more?'

'Why don't you do what you want to do,' I said. I lay down beside him again and the bed creaked as we shifted into position with him on top of me.

'Wait a minute, wait a minute,' I said. I could see him wondering, what now. 'Have you got any protection?'

'Oh,' he panted. 'Protection. Yes.' He looked about him vaguely. 'Yes. Somewhere. Of course. Protection.'

186

He got out of bed and went into the living room and looked towards his books. 'I have one. It is here somewhere. I'll look for it. Don't worry, I'll find it. Just a minute.'

He stood framed in the doorway, and I looked at his erection. A funny thing to have. And they all walk about as if to have it sticking out in front of them was a very serious and necessary thing.

'I hid one in a book somewhere. I had to hide it from my father. So I put it in a book that I knew he wouldn't read. Which one was it? Let me see.'

He began to reach for books, shaking them out and then putting them back again. Everywhere I looked there were books.

'What kind of book? Can you remember?'

'No, I can't.'

'Stop for a minute. Think, think. What kind of book wouldn't he read?'

He stopped and looked at the book case. 'He only reads his subject. Church history.'

'How many books have you got on that?'

'Not so many.'

'So all the rest are your subject?'

'I'll find it, I'll find it.' He began shaking out books again, reaching haphazardly here and there, desperately searching. I got up and joined him, crouching on the floor of the living-room so as not to be seen through the verandah window. He saw me and closed the shutters.

'It's no use,' I said after a while and he stood and looked at me with a book in his hand.

He put it down on the table and I noticed that his erection had gone. His face had fallen too.

'I wasn't prepared,' he said unhappily.

I sat down on the smooth cold cement. He looked at my breasts and his penis began to grow. 'Can I kiss your breasts?' he asked. I nearly said no, but what was the point.

We went back into the bedroom and he sat on the edge of the bed and pulled me down onto his knees facing him. His face was sweaty and absorbed by my breasts, his eyes half closed. He took a breast into his mouth and sucked long and slowly and then went to the other one, sucking from one to the other as if he could never have enough, hugging me closer and closer so that I was pressed up against his erection.

This feeling of hot, slippery skin wet with his tongue and the smell of him too, of his sweat as it trickled down his chest and his back; I felt it on my fingers and rubbed it over his bony back. It had a smell to it that made me think of crowded buses and tired men with long eyelashes who looked at me with a languid curiosity, on their way home to a mysterious life.

His penis was rubbing against my clitoris and it was almost better than doing it myself. I rubbed harder and when I came I tried to do so silently but I couldn't hold it in. It came out in a groan against his shoulder. Just in time too because he reached for his penis and began masturbating, my breasts forgotten, his face between them, his breath hard. He came without a sound. I only knew that it was over when I felt something warm and sticky on one of my breasts.

We stayed unmoving for a while and then I shifted a little.

'I hurt you?' he asked, his voice muffled by my breasts.

'No. No, you didn't hurt me.'

'I thought I did. But I couldn't stop. You are sure?' He lifted his head and looked at me, concerned. Sweat was running down his face.

'Really.'

'Why did you make that sound? It was pain surely.'

'Actually it was pleasure.'

'How is this?' He looked suspicious, as if I were making a fool of him.

The tap in the kitchen was dripping into the sink. I slid off his knees and stood up. We were both wet with sweat and I could feel it trickling down my neck and mingling with his semen. He had a good look at me again as I stood before him, a little unsteady on my feet.

'Shall we wash now?' I said.

'Usually the water is off by now,' he said. 'Let me see.'

He went into the bathroom and turned on a tap and I heard that empty coughing sound of no water coming out of it.

'But the tap in the kitchen is dripping,' I said.

'It does that always, water or not. Don't worry, I have a little put by in a dekchi. Come, wash.'

He came out of the bathroom and indicated to me that I had the place to myself.

'I don't want to use all the water,' I said.

'Please don't worry. I can wait till it comes on again.'

'But that's maybe not for a few hours yet.'

'Please, please,' he said, waving me into the bathroom again.

'Is there not enough for both of us?'

'No, for one only. You must wash.'

I went in and he shut the door behind me. The room was cement grey, cool and dark with a tiny window up by the ceiling. The tin dekchi was on the floor by the tap. I lifted the lid and it was about half full. Why did he only half fill the damn thing? What good is half a dekchi of water to anybody? The lid slid off and clattered on to the floor, echoing loudly.

I heard him open a drawer and wondered if he had his trousers on. He looked apprehensive when I came out. He was sitting on the bed, still naked, a handkerchief in his hand.

'Washed so soon?' he said.

'No,' I said.

'What then?'

'What you were asking before. About pleasure.'

'And?'

'It was pleasure, really.'

He looked at the floor, smiling slightly.

'I'll show you,' I said, and lay down on the bed. 'Look, look.' I touched his slippery back and he turned reluctantly.

'No, down there. You have to see it.'

'See what?'

'Where my finger is.'

He stood at the foot of the bed and leaned down and looked, his face intent. It took a huge effort to keep my legs apart.

'This thing?' he asked.

'Yes. If you rub it then I feel the same way you do, you know, when you get excited and then climax.'

'Like this?' he said, with sudden enthusiasm.

'Not so hard, not so hard.'

'All women have this?'

'Yes. And what's best is if you do it with your tongue.' I'd never managed to say that to anyone before.

'Oh,' he said and continued staring. His finger moved down and then pushed a little up my vagina. He darted a glance at me to see if this was OK and then pushed it right in. He began rhythmically pushing it in and out.

'You like this?' he whispered, smiling slyly and pleased with himself. My heart sank as he climbed on to the bed and knelt down to the job.

But I lay back anyway and felt my legs relax further apart. I don't know; nice men can't fuck.

'It's good. It is good?' he asked, seeing me smile. 'You like?'

The water came on. I was getting very dry. The tap gurgled, spluttered, coughed and spat and produced a thin trickle. I looked towards the bathroom.

'You left the tap on,' I said.

'You want to wash now?'

'I think so.'

'OK. So wash.'

He left me alone again and I was glad of it this time.

26

'DID YOU ASK HIM?' Mum said when I got back. She came over to me, her shoulders hunched and her neck strained forward, half-whispering, looking guilty and excited and giving a little giggle.

'No. Did you?'

'He's in the bathroom. He's not long up. But I'm not going to. I don't think I could. It wouldn't be right.' She turned away and looked at the floor.

'No, it wouldn't. You're right.' Dad swished water in the bathroom sink. 'That's why I didn't ask Rahul.'

'Did you have a nice time?'

My breasts were throbbing. 'Yes.'

'You look as though you have.'

'We had fun,' I said, and Mum smiled a little sadly.

'I want you to have fun. I want you to have lots of fun before you go. I'm just going to make tea,' she said and started towards the kitchen. But when Dad came out of the bathroom, she turned abruptly and went into the bedroom, shutting the door behind her.

'Are you making tea?' Dad asked me.

We made tea together. He filled the kettle and I got the cups and saucers on a tray and carried them on to the back verandah. As I was pouring tea, the front door slammed.

'I'll go after her,' I said.

'Yes, all right.'

I caught up with her at the gate. 'Where are you going?'

'He just sits there,' she said. 'Just sits there.'

'What should he do?'

'I don't know. Something. Not as if nothing has happened.'

'Get angry at him then.'

'I will. You bet I will.'

'Go back now. Say it to him now.'

'No, I'll see Padma first.'

She strode on. I noticed she was carrying her bag and wondered if she planned on running away to Calcutta again.

There was a huge noise coming from the servants' quarters, shrieking and yelling and threatening. As soon as Mum heard it she ran up the road.

A crowd of women was under the tree where the men usually sat. Mum pushed her way into the centre and two women stood with blood running down their faces. One had a stick in her hand and the other was holding a long metal spoon. Their hair was all over their faces. Mum grabbed one of them by her arm and pulled the stick out of her hand.

'Who are you?' she shouted. 'I don't know any of you. Who are you?' She looked around the crowd. 'I don't know who you are, but you don't belong here. This is our home. Who are you that you think you can come here and make trouble?'

'It wasn't me, Memsahib,' said the one with the spoon. She was young and tough-looking. 'It was her. You ask her. Go on, ask her. See what she says.'

'It wasn't me who did it, it was her, throwing her rubbish in front of my door.' She was much older and shrewish.

'That's where the rubbish goes, that's where she throws it herself, living like a pig, outside her own door.'

'It's my door and I'll do what I like outside my own door. Just let me get at you and I'll throw you in it, I'll stick your face in it, you filthy whore.' She pushed Mum aside and grabbed the woman's hair and began pulling her towards the houses. The crowd started shouting again. Mum grabbed the hair of the older one and pulled her to the ground. She turned on the one standing and pulled her down as well.

192

'I want you out of here,' she shouted. 'All of you. I don't know who you are but you have no right to be here.'

The women looked up at her with sullen eyes.

'I'm family,' the younger one said. The older one stood up and tried to get her stick back from Mum's hand.

'Who?' Mum said. 'Whose family?'

'Anukal's.'

'How are you Anukal's family?'

'I'm his wife's sister.'

'His wife doesn't have a sister,' Mum said.

'I'm his wife's sister,' she insisted. 'I've come to take care of the baby while his wife is ill. It's this one, this one, she has no right here.'

'His wife isn't ill. I spoke to her yesterday. Don't lie to me.'

'It's not a lie, Memsahib. Are you calling me a liar?'

'Yes, I am. And who are you?' Mum asked the other one.

'I'm from Seema's family,' the older one said in a whining voice. 'His brother is my husband's cousin. We're buying a cow.'

'So you're buying a cow,' Mum said. 'That doesn't give you the right to live here.'

'Memsahib, we're buying a cow from Seema's mother. We have to come here to make the arrangements. We're going away tomorrow.' She gave an ingratiating grin.

'Where is this rubbish?' Mum demanded.

'Here, Memsahib here, I'll show you, right outside my door,' the younger one said.

The crowd was huge now. Rickshaw men stood with folded arms and discussed the issues. We followed the women to a mound of rubbish. Mum stood with her hands on her hips and looked at it.

'You live here,' she said. 'Why do you leave your rubbish here like this?'

'She does it.'

'Everyone does it. I can see that. Don't I have eyes? What do you think I am, stupid? I don't want any more of your lies. I'm going to come back in two day's time and if you're still here

193

I'm calling the police. Do you understand?' She turned angrily to one woman and then the other.

'Yes, Memsahib,' they said.

'And anyone else who shouldn't be here. I'm going to go around all your houses and I'm going to find out everything. Go back to your villages. This is our home, not yours. You leave us alone. There's nothing here for you.' She tossed the stick onto the rubbish pile.

The crowd was silent and as she turned away they began muttering.

'What is it?' she said, turning on them. 'What are you saying?'

'Nothing, Memsahib. We're not saying anything,' an old man said.

When we returned, Dad was still drinking tea. 'Where have you been?' he asked calmly, as if we'd just popped out to the shops.

27

O N CHRISTMAS MORNING THE bell rang. Roshan answered it while we were having breakfast.

'It's the egg man,' he said and stood beside Dad and waited.

'Oh dear,' Dad said, looking at Mum. 'Oh dear, oh dear.'

She put her cup down. 'What'll we do?'

'About what?' I asked.

But they continued looking at each other. 'Is there nothing in the drawer?' Mum asked.

'It's all accounted for,' Dad said.

'And you didn't get any extra? I told you to get extra.'

'There wasn't any extra to get. There's nothing left. We're completely out.'

'We'll have to give somebody less.'

'We can't do that,' Dad said. 'Who would we give less to?'

'I don't know,' Mum said crossly. 'Have you any better ideas?'

Dad tapped his lips with his forefinger. He turned to Roshan. 'Ask him to wait a few minutes, please.'

Roshan went to the door, growled something, and then shut it.

'It's all my fault,' Mum said. 'I should have remembered the egg man.'

'It doesn't matter whose fault it is,' Dad said irritably. 'It's what we're going to do about it that matters.'

The egg man was a droopy Christian who had fallen on hard times. Mum and Dad had given him some money to set up his egg selling business and every week he came round with tiny little eggs to sell. Today he'd come for a Christmas tip.

'Bheme hasn't been round yet,' Dad said. 'If we told him that we'd give him his tip in a few weeks' time, maybe he wouldn't mind.'

'No, I don't want to do that to Bheme,' Mum said. 'Not with Sarasati and the baby. Maybe they can't wait. We don't know.'

'Well, who then?'

'Haven't you got any money at all?' I asked.

'None whatsoever,' Dad said, spreading his hands.

'I've got just enough to see us through till the pay comes in January,' Mum said. 'If it comes in time. Maybe we could give him something instead of money.'

I got up as they talked about jerseys and scarves and shirts. I went to my bag, took out twenty rupees and went to the front door. The man was leaning against the wall and his ingratiating look faded when he saw it was me.

'Happy Christmas,' I said in English and gave him the money.

He shook his head sideways. 'Happy Christmas,' he muttered. 'Mummy no there?'

'She's busy now. It's a busy day.'

'Busy day. Yes,' he said and looked over my shoulder into the flat.

There was a pause and he looked down at his money, then shook his head sideways again and left, his feet dragging on the stairs.

Back inside they had nearly decided, hesitating between Dad's green jersey, which he wanted to give to someone in the mountains, and his blue one which had a hole in the elbow and Mum wanted to mend.

'I've paid him,' I said.

'Who?' Mum asked.

'The egg man. I gave him twenty rupees.'

'That's far too much,' Dad said.

'Oh fuck off,' I said and sat down to finish my coffee.

I heard him scratch his cheek, his nail rasping against his skin.

'A jersey is worth far more than twenty rupees,' Mum said.

'That's not the point,' Dad said. 'The point –.'

'What is the point?' Mum asked.

'That we've got to be fair,' he said, insistently, leaning towards her. 'What is the use of carefully counting out all the rupee notes if one of them gets twice what the others do?'

Dad cycled to the bank every year to get brand new rupee notes for the servants' tips. They liked this. Look, they said to me afterwards. He always gives us new notes.

'I don't think you've any room to talk about giving money,' Mum said.

'What do you mean by that?'

'You know perfectly well what I mean.'

'No, I don't. I don't know anything of the kind.'

'Giving money to the police,' she said. Her cheeks were bright red.

'Oh,' Dad said, putting his hands together in his lap and looking down at them, as if he had completely forgotten about that.

'It's all right for you to bribe, but not for Hannah to give someone too much money in a tip.'

'Don't confuse the two issues,' he said. 'They're completely different.'

'No, they're not. They're just the same.'

'How are they the same? How?'

'I don't know. They just are.'

'That's no argument. You must know what you're trying to say.' His eyes were grey and hard. She looked at the table. He glared at her.

'Fuck off,' she said.

It sounded wrong in her mouth, feeble and weak, a last tottering stand.

Dad gave a little snort.

'I'm saying you were wrong, you shouldn't have done such a thing without asking me first,' she said.

'Where do you come into it?' he said.

'Oh God!' I cried. 'What an awful fucking country this is! What a fucking awful country.'

There was a silence. Dad stared at his hands, then at his plate. He raised his head and caught my eye. 'It must be time for church,' he said.

Mum didn't move.

'I suppose I was wrong to give the money,' he said.

'Yes,' Mum said. 'You were.' She got up. 'Have you done your face?' she asked me. 'I've just got to do mine, then I'll be ready. Let's hope the service isn't too long.'

'It's always long on Christmas day,' I said.

'And boring,' Dad said.

'Who's taking it?'

'Mr Ramamurthy.'

We all groaned. 'She should have sucked his blood and been done with it,' Mum called from the bedroom. 'Then we'd have had a nicer Christmas.'

Dad laughed and stood with his hands in his pockets and waited for her.

We walked out of our compound and towards the main gate. The rickshaw men saw us coming and two of them slapped a cloth around the seats in readiness. 'Congratulations on your big day,' they said.

Instead of climbing on, Dad looked at the rickshaw. 'It is a pretty bloody awful place,' he said quietly. 'Of course, it's loving it that's the problem.'

Apart from his sermons, this was the only time I'd heard him use the word love. I opened my mouth to reply and a man hurried past us, soaking wet from praying in the filthy river. 'Congratulations on your big day,' he said. He smiled, showing small white teeth and high cheekbones.

'Thank you,' I said.

'Who was that?' Mum asked.

'My cigarette man,' I said. He'd never spoken to me before.

In the afternoon we left the flat to go to the children's tea party on the playing-fields across from Anjali's house. There were tables laid out with food and a crowd of excited children running about, with clean shirts and dresses and wet hair. Adults milled around too, keeping an eye on them, making sure they didn't touch the food. But the children weren't interested. They were waiting for Father Christmas to come and kept running up along the side of the library and running back with the news. Not here yet, not here.

'Who is Father Christmas this year?' I asked. All the men were present that I could see, and Rahul too who smiled at me. It was a smile that said, look at us now and look how we were. I hoped he wouldn't join us.

'Wait and see,' Mum said.

'Go on. Who is it?'

'I'm not telling you.'

'Do you know, Dad?'

'I'm not telling you either.'

A Naga woman with a big face came up to us. She wasn't pretty like the other ones, but her face was alive with interest and pleasure. It was Nudy Hemrom, Mr Ramamurthy's least favourite student. She took my arm.

'You have a lovely daughter,' she said to Mum. 'We were just saying, you have a lovely daughter.'

Mum took my other arm. 'Yes, I do,' she said.

'When are you going home?' the Naga woman asked me.

'I don't know,' I said. 'Soon.'

'Your mother will be sad.'

'Very sad,' Mum said.

'You must come and see us then,' she said to her. 'We will make you happy again.'

'I'll do that,' Mum said. 'I'll do that.'

The Naga woman laughed, her eyes almost disappearing into her face, and she let my arm go and went back to her friends.

'So you're going soon?' Dad said.

'I thought I would.'

'I see.'

I waited for him to say something else but I guess he figured Mum had done all the talking.

A rickshaw came round the corner of the library heading for us, and the children let out a shriek. A figure, round and jovial and also a little uncertain, sat in it wearing a red robe and a white beard; there was a huge sack on the floor of the rickshaw. The rickshaw driver was wearing his usual lungi and shirt and he pedalled slowly, bearing his burden with gravity. Father Christmas held on to the seat with one hand to stop being bumped out and waved with the other. The children waved back, a little subdued by this extraordinary figure.

'It's Mrs Kershaw!' I said, and Mum laughed.

'None of the men would do it,' she said.

Mrs Kershaw cried 'Ho, ho, ho,' from her rickshaw. The man brought her to a stop in front of the crowd of children and they all took a step back as she got off awkwardly. Dad went to help her lift the sack down and students pushed the children into lines, one for girls, one for boys.

'Do I need a man?' I asked Mum.

I don't need a man. 'Why did I think I did? They're more trouble than they're worth. And the world seemed a lighter place.

Mum watched pensively as the children shyly received their gifts. A baby on a girl's hip howled in terror. 'You take care of yourself,' she said. 'Because I love you. You know that, don't you.'

'Yes, I know.'

'I love you very much.'

'I know.'

'Sometimes a man can make you happy,' she said.

Anjali and Lucky came running from their house across the playing-field towards us. Anjali was holding Lucky's hand, trying to make her run faster to be in time to get her present. But wee Lucky had her finger pressed on the bridge of her nose to keep her sunglasses on. She tripped and fell and Anjali picked her up, brushed her dress down and rubbed her knees. She handed her the sunglasses and took her hand again and they carried on running.